SPACE TAKERS

SPACE TAKERS
AN ORIGIN STORY

Megan Cain

Geek
STREET

ISBN: 979-8-218-37153-1

For true friends

I've only had a handful
And I think of you still

CONTENTS

CONTENTS

The Rise of Fruit Man

Something Heroic

"A Hair-Raising Demise"

That's what the clickbait headline would read. Or maybe "Tresses of Terror Pulverize Preteens." That definitely had a ring to it.

Helen's head hurt. She was dazed, but remembered that she and Cathy had been in a collision. Neck straining, she tried to look around. Where was Cathy? What about Danni and Kat? They had been right behind her.

A loud *crack* penetrated the still air. Helen looked up at the tree they had collided with as it swayed and groaned above them. The force of the impact had splintered the bark and now, the old tree was barely standing upright. It tilted forward and caught on some of the smaller trees around it.

"It's gonna fall!" Kat yelled.

For all her confusion and pain, Helen could have been in a car accident, but she wasn't surrounded by twisted metal and broken glass. Instead, the ground was a deep mahogany red with hair that rippled and writhed across the leaf litter. Helen

1

was tangled up in it and Cathy was lost somewhere beneath its twisting locks. Helen's scalp ached from where she had been yanked off her feet. She could hardly believe that all this mess was coming from her own head.

Kat came to her side and tugged at her arm, snapping Helen from her confusion. She struggled to free herself from the tangled mess around her. Several feet away, Danni was likewise trying to free Cathy—a wriggling lump beneath the waves.

"It's-con-stric-ting-me!" Cathy choked.

Three thoughts crossed Helen's mind as she laid there on the forest floor, waiting to be crushed. The first was how absurd she and her friends must look, trying to free themselves from a giant knot of hair as the forest came down around them.

A large branch snapped and came crashing down next to Kat. She ducked to the side, narrowly missing death, as red tresses entwined themselves around her ankles. Danni parted through sections of hair to search for Cathy, who had still not surfaced. Tufts of hair climbed her forearms with each digging motion.

"Helen! Get control of your hair!" she yelled.

Helen's second thought was that this whole disaster was all her fault. Besides the obvious fact that the crimson hair attacking everyone was hers, none of them would have even been here if she had not convinced them to come. In fact, none of these strange occurrences would even be happening if it hadn't been for her.

A second tree broke, and the old oak no longer had anything substantial to keep it upright. It creaked and groaned as it fell forward, showering the four girls with snapping twigs and branches. Its shadow blocked the waning light and Helen froze, filled with horror. She was only twelve years old. And she was about to die.

The final thought, as several tons of tree trunk fell over her vision, was of her friends. Were they thinking the same thing? Were they blaming her as well? Kat, the girl she barely knew. Danni, her new friend and gym class partner. And her best friend, Cathy. Poor Cathy. Were the past few weeks flashing before her eyes, too?

UNLIKELY
FRIENDS

CHAPTER ONE
"There seems to be some mistake"

Cathy

Cathy Gutiérrez-Guttenberg stood ten paces back from the two chatty girls climbing onto the bus ahead of her. She took a seat in the middle while they continued straight to the back.

As the bus pulled forward, Cathy took her breakfast from her backpack, doing her best to remain inconspicuous. She ducked down and hovered over the zipper to cushion the sound of crinkling plastic. Discretion was difficult when you were the heavy girl who ate cupcakes for breakfast.

She had started out her morning by making herself an egg and cheese biscuit, but her younger brother had stolen it from the microwave while her back was turned. Their mother had been no help at all.

On the phone with Tita, she had said, "Just get another one, mija."

Well, it was the last one. And Lenny never got in trouble for anything.

Cathy could still see Lenny's gloating gaze. He had chewed exaggeratedly as he watched her search the kitchen for something else. When their mother told Tita how great Lenny would do in soccer this year, Cathy had had enough. She had grabbed a chocolaty cupcake snack pack from above the fridge (which was covered in Lucy's latest artwork) before scooping up her bookbag and hurrying out the door with her brother's praises still ringing in her ears.

Cathy wasn't athletic like Lenny, or creative like Lucy, but soon, she would get to spend the day in her own element. She had high grades in school, the praise of her teachers, and the camaraderie of her classmates—but her report cards never went on the fridge, and at home, she felt left out.

She heard a snort from the aisle next to her. The bus had made its next stop and Tina Haggleman had seen the cupcakes. Tina slipped into the seat across the aisle and gestured for her friends to come up from the back.

Feeling left out on the bus wouldn't be so bad.

Idelle Jeffries sat down behind Tina, and Priscilla Driscalle stopped to stare directly at Cathy, appraising her like she was livestock. Cathy knew she was about to get eaten alive. She slipped the cupcakes back into her bag.

8

Priscilla slid next to Tina as the bus growled forward again. Cathy looked out the window. Inconspicuous was off the table, so she concentrated on the sounds of the bus instead, trying to ignore the conversation in the seats next to her.

"Cici, did you see what she's wearing?"

"Oh, I saw."

Cathy shifted her backpack from the floor to the seat beside her, a crude privacy screen. She knew her clothes weren't perfect, but she hadn't chosen them. Their parents had taken Lucy shopping for a brand-new wardrobe for high school, which meant brand-new *old* clothes for Cathy.

She and Lucy looked so much alike. They had the same curly dark hair and dimpled cheeks, the same wide brown eyes and tawny skin. Only, Cathy was stuck with glasses and she was bigger around the waist, despite being three years younger. It was her first year of middle school, and she didn't get a new wardrobe. She got hand-me-downs. The clothes were pilled from too many washes and the styles were creative, like Lucy. They barely fit, and they bore the tinge of the label, "hand-me-downs."

After a few minutes, Priscilla and her friends moved on from criticizing Cathy to complimenting each other's fashion choices. Cathy was able to relax for the rest of the ride, letting her empty stomach complain to itself. Lunch was three periods away.

When the bus arrived, the front of the school was bustling with students. They crammed through the doors to get to their lockers and classes. Cathy sorted notebooks and binders in her own locker before heading for room 210.

Another student already sat at one of the desks and, finally, Cathy's day was looking up.

Her best friend, Helen, rested with her feet up on the chair next to her. A tired expression drooped from her lightly freckled face, and her head hung back as if she had been sleeping. Her long red hair brushed the ground.

The sight of Helen made Cathy feel better about her morning. Even though Helen refused to be in a good mood at any time before ten o'clock, Cathy could see the sly twinkle at the corner of her friend's eye and a hint of the constant smirk she wore, as if the whole world was a secret joke in Helen's mind.

"Welcome to the marvelous world of math class," Helen Hughes yawned, "with everybody's favorite teacher..."

Without lifting her head, she held up her schedule and squinted at it.

"Ms. Gryz—Gryzicks—Gryzicksva? Hey, look at that, Cathy. Someone with a last name that's more of a mouthful than yours."

Helen

Three class periods later, Helen and Cathy were the first in line for lunch. Helen clutched a crumpled wad of dollar bills and considered her options. The standard school meal taunted her, oozing and crusting, an insult to the milk carton next to it.

"Not gonna happen," she said.

Instead, Helen chose a wrapped peanut butter and jelly sandwich, a bag of chips, and a fizzy drink from the cooler below. Cathy took one of the trays of steamy food. Her parents didn't give her money to spend. Cathy had an account instead.

"What even is that?" Helen asked.

"Lasagna and mashed potatoes," Cathy muttered.

"What a disgusting combination."

"You're not helping, Helen."

"Garçon!" Helen shouted and snapped her fingers.

"Shh!" Cathy giggled. "Helen!"

"Excuse me, garçon! Yes, my friend here ordered the Asian bistro lunch, and there seems to be some mistake. You see, what we have here is a conglomeration of Italian and southern home cooking. I demand you take it back at once!"

Cathy had to stifle her laughter for fear of dropping her lunch tray. Helen had been trying to cheer her up all day. Even though Cathy had brushed it off, it was obvious she had had a bad morning.

"Pssst!"

"What was that?" Cathy looked around.

"I dunno," Helen said. "What was what?"

"You got us in trouble!"

"Pssssssssstttt!"

They flinched at the giant-sized horn-rimmed glasses and the frizzy mass of salt-and-pepper hair that had been hiding behind the sneeze guard. Helen and Cathy exchanged glances before leaning in to acknowledge the lunch lady.

"The sneeze guard only works one way," Helen said. "Stop pssst-ing at us."

"Are we in trouble?" Cathy asked in a strained voice.

The lunch lady's over-magnified eyes shifted from left to right. "Don't get the school lunch," she whispered.

Helen played along, whispering behind her hand conspiratorially. "She can't help it. She has to."

"It comes from a box…" the shifty eyes insisted.

Helen scoffed. "Why doesn't that surprise me?"

The lunch lady snatched Cathy by the wrist and Cathy almost dropped her tray again.

"They lie!" the lunch lady said. "The box—it can't contain them—they grow."

Cathy squirmed in her discomfort, but the crazed lunch lady continued.

"They neeeed the gravy."

Helen leaned around Cathy's shoulder. "It's okay. She doesn't liiiike the gravy—"

Not dissuaded, the lady pulled Cathy closer. "I watched them make it, toil and trouble. The gravy's almost done!"

One lens on Cathy's glasses fogged up, either from the food vats or the lunch lady's much-too-close-for-comfort breath.

"H-Helen?" Cathy squeaked.

Helen glimpsed the lunch lady's nametag as she bent over the steamy vats of food.

"Hey Linda, watch out!" Helen pointed. "That kid's getting potatoes, too!"

"No!" Linda dropped Cathy's wrist. "Boy! Little boy!"

Helen seized the opportunity to usher her friend out of the creepy zone, leaving Linda to harass the next kid in line.

Once they made it past the cash registers, she asked Cathy, "What. On earth. Was that?"

Cathy scrutinized her tray. "Is it safe to eat?"

Helen looked back at the crazed cafeteria worker—who had scared away the next kid and taken to arguing with the peach cobbler.

"Yeah, I think you're good to go."

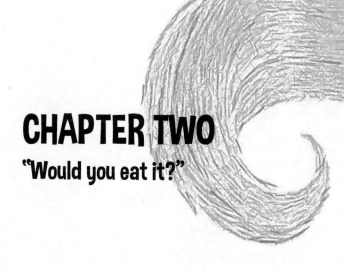

CHAPTER TWO

"Would you eat it?"

Danni

Danni Emerson moved like a missile, locked on to her target. She dodged and spun—a linebacker, sidestepping the hungry students who got in her way. Danni Emerson was on a mission. Her hair was still neat, even after gym class. She was dressed in her best outfit and she homed in on the round table at the middle of the cafeteria—the one where Priscilla had assembled her group of admiring devotees. Priscilla Driscalle, the daughter of Daphne Driscalle, the style influencer! Starstruck, Danni knew she belonged at that table.

She had identified them in class last period—a group of like-minded girls she could talk to about fashion and gossip, a large network of friends to get acquainted with this year.

There was one chair open. One chair left at the table of style. Danni had style. The spot would be hers. As she neared the table, Danni produced her widest, friendliest smile. She stopped short of the chair, blocking it to the throng of other newcomers who were, no doubt, waiting their turns to apply for greatness. The group eyeballed her quizzically.

Perhaps her smile was too big. Perhaps it was scary, even. Her confidence cracked.

"Hey, Priscilla!" she said in an awkward shout.

Play it cool, Danni thought. She relaxed her face and spoke more casually. "I mean, what's up, Cici?"

"Hi...?" came Priscilla's confused response.

"Danni," whispered one of the groupies.

"Hi, Danni." Priscilla said, a wry curl on her glossy pink lips. "I'm trying to eat my lunch. What's up with you?"

As she spoke, Priscilla brushed her jet-black hair away from the corner of her eye. It was the kind of brush that wasn't meant to keep hair out of eyes—like putting it behind her ear, which *of course*, would look *so* common. What she accomplished instead was to highlight the striking amber of her iris, her high cheekbone, and pointed chin. Danni noted that a.) this was done on purpose, b.) it was an acquired skill, and c.) Priscilla would have to become her best friend so they could share with each other all the delightful little tips and tricks they knew. As her hand came to rest under her chin, Priscilla watched Danni with amused eyes, waiting.

15

Danni pictured the two of them in her room, practicing looks in the mirror together, cute pouts, and judgmental side-eyes.

"I was wondering," Danni said, "if you don't mind, if I could sit with you guys."

Priscilla's voice was sickly sweet, "Yeah…I'm afraid there isn't any room left for you."

"Oh." Danni lifted her hands from the back of the chair she had been leaning on. They must have been saving it for someone. She masked her disappointment with pleasantry, "That's okay. Maybe next time."

One of Priscilla's friends chuckled. "Yeah, maybe."

Danni resolved to find a seat elsewhere, telling herself not to be offended by what had happened. It was only a minor upset, so far. A voice called her name and Danni looked over her shoulder.

"Love your pants, by the way!" Priscilla cooed.

"Aw, thanks!" Danni walked away with her head held high.

Cathy

Having escaped the lunch line, Helen and Cathy stood at the mouth of a large middle aisle, scanning the cafeteria for a place to eat.

"So, where are we sitting?" Cathy asked.

Still holding her tray, Helen head-motioned, "With her."

They made their way through the crowd to the middle of a long table, where a tall girl with a deep umber complexion sat by herself, dumping out the contents of a purple lunch bag. She looked up as they set their trays on her table.

"Hey, Danni," Helen said, "this is Cathy. Cathy, this is Danni."

"Hi," Danni said.

Danni had her short black hair pulled up into a small, tight bun and she wore a flowy patterned top, earrings, and a dangly necklace. Her appearance was so polished that Cathy felt uncomfortable in her presence. Cathy juggled her tray and her backpack so she could free a hand to tug her own shirt down, in case it was wrinkled or riding up.

"I met Danni in gym class, last period," Helen continued, as they took their seats. "She helped me clean some old gunk out of the locker they assigned me. I think this gym uniform stuff is weird."

Danni's light brown eyes were inviting.

"I thought you said you were going to sit with Priscilla at lunch," Helen said.

"You're friends with Priscilla?" Cathy asked, a red flag flapping in her mind.

"We're not exactly best friends." Danni was quick to add, "We could be. Maybe. Eventually. She likes my pants, you know—"

The sound of an air raid siren quieted the cafeteria and everyone turned to the stage, where a wiry man in a brown suit and glasses held a megaphone in the air. He brought it to his lips and spoke.

"Good morning students of Percival P. Pearson Middle School. And welcome new sixth graders! For those of you who don't know me yet, I am Principal Paloski—"

"WOOO! Principal Pal and his bullhorn!" an eighth grader shouted from the back of the room.

The gathered students found this amusing, but the megaphone quieted the room once again with an ear-shattering air horn.

"As I was saying," the principal spoke into the megaphone, "I am Principal Jason Paloski—or, Principal Pal if you like. I want to work together to make this a spectacular school year—the best year yet for PPP! Some of you may have noticed the brand-new vending machines this year." Students cheered and applauded. "These machines are a reward, so long as everything progresses in a calm and orderly fashion. So, let's be on our best behavior everyone, and welcome back to Pearson!"

He stepped briskly off the stage and the cafeteria resumed its previous activity.

Cathy dug around in her backpack and pulled out her cupcakes and a small wallet. "I'll be back in a sec."

Helen and Danni joked about their gym locker experience as Cathy wove her way to the vending machines. She could pick at what she had had to buy from the lunch line, but she was super hungry after skipping breakfast. As she waited for the machine to drop her item, Cathy caught movement from the corner of her eye. A lone girl leaned against the wall, quietly ignoring the rest of the lunch room. If the girl hadn't moved her arm, Cathy would have missed her entirely.

The girl finished taking a swig of her soda and stared back at Cathy. She wore baggy black pants and a dark grey shirt with hot pink netting that covered the sleeves. Her mid-length blonde hair was braided back on one side, and she had pale skin to match it. As Cathy observed her, the girl's expression switched to annoy-ance, an easy shift with her thin arched eyebrows.

"Was there something?" she asked.

"Uh, cool shirt?"

The girl scowled at Cathy with piercing blue eyes. "Okay... Thanks?"

"Are you going to eat that, just leaning there?" Cathy asked, referring to the bag of chips in the girl's hand. "Because we've got extra seats."

She was amazed at herself for being so bold and imitating Helen, who could strike up a conversation with anyone. *Look Helen, I can find a new friend too!*

The girl shrugged. "I guess it's better than standing here all period."

"I prefer to lie down," Cathy blurted, "and be lazier—which is way c-cool...Uh, this way."

"Second thought."

"No no no! C'mon," said Cathy. "We have all the seats!"

Cathy resisted the urge to smack herself in the forehead. She led the way to their table, followed by this new girl, who paused, unsure of what to do next.

"What took you so long?" Helen asked before noticing that Cathy had a follower. "Oh," she said. "Hi."

"Yeah! This is…uh…" Cathy felt stupid.

"Kat," said the girl. "I didn't have a seat."

"That's short for Katherine, right?" Cathy asked. "That's my name, too! Kind of. But in Spanish. I go by Cathy."

"Wait, what's your name?" Danni asked.

"Catalina, so Cathy, get it?"

"And you're Kat?"

Kat nodded.

Danni shook her head. "I feel like you guys should be switched. Kathy for Katherine, and Cat for Catalina?"

"My dad came up with the nicknames…" Cathy muttered.

Kat lowered herself into a chair, slow and careful, as if she would bolt at any moment. With a nervous chuckle, Cathy made a mental note to study hard in science, go to college for engineering, get her doctorate in advanced physics, invent the time machine, go back to five minutes ago, and never be bold again.

Outgoing as always, Helen took over. "I'm Helen, by the way, and this is Danni."

"Is that a Samurai Lizard on your shirt?" Kat asked her.

"You recognize Picasso?" Helen said. "Great minds think alike. I wear my favorite shirt and find a fellow YSLF fan!"

"Never said I was a fan."

"In fact," Helen ignored, "Danni was just telling me about how her pants are the key to school-wide popularity."

Kat tilted back to view this special article of clothing. She sat up and told Danni, "You have a stain on your leg."

Danni's gaze shot down to her lap.

Kat added, "Looks like jelly."

Danni grabbed her napkin and scrubbed her leg with it, vigorously trying to clean five-hour-old grape stains with a dry paper towel.

"It must have been my sister's fault, at breakfast! Jasmine, you little snot!"

Then she stopped. Mortified at the realization, she dropped her head to the table with a loud bump.

"Love your pants..." she mumbled.

"Maybe Priscilla has a good sense of humor?" Helen offered.

"Priscilla? Driscalle?" Kat chortled. "Right."

Danni changed the subject, eager to end her embarrassment. "Hey, why did you go to the vending machine if you already have food?"

Cathy braced herself for the oncoming ridicule. Cue the fat jokes in three, two, one...

"Would you eat it?" Helen jumped in. "School lunch is so gross. I dare anyone to eat it."

At that, Kat thrust her finger into the mound of Cathy's mashed potatoes and scooped a bite into her mouth. Her face shifted from smug to disgusted.

"That's brave," said Danni, "and a little gross, to put your finger in someone else's food…"

Not to be outdone, Helen snagged herself a glop of Cathy's potatoes, too.

"What's it like?" Cathy was sickened.

"Try it," came Kat's muffled response. She seemed to be having trouble choking it down.

"Yeah," Helen spoke with her mouth still full. "It'll be the potato pact."

Kat swallowed. "That's dumb."

"I'm not suggesting we walk around with bracelets and matching T-shirts. It was a joke." Helen made a mock-mystified face and wiggled her fingers as if she were casting a spell. In a wavering voice she said, "It's not like we'll be bound together by the eating of mashed potatoes."

Cathy and Danni inspected the tray of food, but neither made a move.

"C'mon, Danni, you're a bagged-luncher! You've got no idea how this junk tastes," Helen goaded. "And you bought it, Cathy. You might as well eat some of it."

Cathy's and Danni's eyes met: *I will if you will.*

Both Cathy and Danni pinched off a bite, but Danni paused. "What do I get if I do this?"

Helen was quick to answer, mischievous eyes sparkling. "The satisfaction of experiencing the same thing we did. It's unforgettable, I assure you."

"Heh," Kat chuckled.

Danni was cautious, but as she dropped a nip of the substance into her own mouth, so did Cathy.

The mashed potatoes launched an immediate assault, not only on Cathy's taste buds, but on her teeth and gums and tonsils. It was a force to be reckoned with, like some sentient something, invading her mouth. It clung to the roof, combating her tongue, and each successful swallow was a small battle her throat wished she hadn't won. Cathy gagged. Danni coughed.

Helen leaned forward. "Well?"

Cathy said the first thing that came to mind. "Very. Gross."

Everyone laughed.

"Okay, but seriously, how is anybody else eating this?" Danni asked.

The others looked around at their fellow lunch-goers.

"She did say they needed gravy," Cathy said. "Maybe it tastes better that way?" She was glad she still had chocolate cupcakes to make up for the experience.

Several minutes later, the trash was cleared and the cafeteria tensed, waiting for the bell to ring with the changing of periods. Helen asked the others where they were headed next.

"Elective," came the unanimous response.

Kat and Helen to art, Danni and Cathy to band. The bell rang, and there was an explosion of sound as chairs scuffed the floor and bookbags scraped against tables—the instant chatter of the mass exodus of students leaving the lunch room. The girls said their good-byes and got up to leave. Kat and Danni parted immediately, but Cathy stopped Helen before going to class.

"Thanks for interrupting the fat joke."

"The what?" Helen asked. "Oh. Come on, I don't think Danni's like that."

"I think she wants to be."

CHAPTER THREE
"You and your potato pact"

Kat

Kat's teacher stood over her. "Miss Crenshaw, I highly doubt that you have enough history knowledge to get out of attending my class. You're only in sixth grade."

"That's right. I'm in sixth grade. What's your excuse?" Kat crossed her arms. "I mean, if you're so great at history, why aren't you working in a museum somewhere? You know, where it's okay to be this boring."

The rest of the class "oohed" at this and the blood rose in Mrs. Francis's cheeks. She wrung her dry erase marker with white knuckles. The plastic cap squeaked under the pressure. Kat had Mrs. Francis right where she wanted her.

"Miss Crenshaw, you are out of line."

Kat scoffed. "Don't call me 'Miss Crenshaw.' I'm not my mother."

Mrs. Francis pursed her lips and squinted at her opponent. Kat met her gaze fearlessly. Had the history classroom been the wild west, a tumbleweed would have blown between them.

If Kat played her cards right, she would get to go home early.

"Are you trying to get a detention on your first day of school?"

Kat opened her mouth to answer, but before she could spew her snarky response, she spewed a stream of neon vomit instead.

. . . .

Kat found the nurse's office, clutching the yellow teacher's pass Mrs. Francis had all too gladly written out for her. Her stomach flip-flopped as she opened the door.

The nurse hummed while doing paperwork at her desk. She sat up and smiled when Kat approached, revealing the hearts and emojis she had been drawing in the margins of important-looking documents.

"Welcome! I'm Nurse Beaux-Baxter," she said in a thick North Central accent. "What's the problem with you?"

Without saying anything, Kat handed the slip of paper to the nurse.

"Oh, another vomitter. Vomitters go over on the left." She pointed. "Pick a cot and I'll be right with you."

Kat turned the corner and her shoulders slumped.

"Hi…" Helen, Cathy, and Danni said in unison.

They waved half-heartedly. Her new companions reclined on separate cots, each face a different shade of green. Cathy sat with a small trash can between her legs. Helen's and Danni's were both on the floor.

Kat sighed, "Great."

"I like her," Helen said, "She's sarcastic."

"So, you speak the same language." Cathy said.

Danni leaned over and threw up.

"Holy buckets! All these children with the first day jitters!" The nurse strode into the room, holding a plastic tub and a bottle of fizzy soda. "You can go back to class now, Tommy," she said to a small boy in the corner. "Be a gentleman and make room for a girl to sit here."

Tommy heaved.

Nurse Beau-Baxter scrunched up her nose and lifted a lavender face mask. "Take the trash can with you, sweetie."

The little kid reluctantly got up, hugging the small bin to his chest. As he hobbled away, Nurse Beaux-Baxter ushered Kat to his seat and gave her the tub and the bottle of soda.

"Drink this. A warm pop to settle your tummy." She peeled a sticker from a sheet in one of her bulging pockets and stuck it to Kat's arm. It was the biohazard image. "Don't mind that, now, dearie." The nurse consulted the other girls, digging in a different pocket. "Now, which one of you got her first menses?"

Helen grimaced. "Wrong side of the room, Nurse B.B."

"Oh! Silly me!"

Nurse Beaux-Baxter strode away again to annoy some poor, poor girl on the other side of the office and Danni whispered, "I don't think she's all there."

"What was your first clue?" Kat asked.

Helen puked into her bucket. She wiped her mouth, "So, what are you here for, Kat?"

"Funny." Kat retched.

"You and your potato pact," coughed Danni.

Helen lifted her bucket and tilted it toward Danni. "Does this look like potatoes to you?"

In response, Danni wrinkled her nose and upchucked again.

"Actually," Cathy studied her trash can with scrunched brows. "This doesn't look like anything I ate today...or ever."

All the girls examined their respective receptacles. Then, they lifted their heads, worried.

"Should it be glowing?" Kat asked.

When the bell rang for the end of school, doors banged open against hallway walls and hundreds of feet pounded on the floors.

"Oh, goodie!" Nurse Beaux-Baxter exclaimed. "Time to go home to my Fuzzkins."

She gathered the papers on her desk, snatched her purse and jacket from a hook on the wall, and dashed for the door, turning out the lights and leaving the sickly students in their gloom.

Helen's voice rasped in the dark. "Oh, isn't this keen."

Kat

A cawing crow announced to the neighborhood that Kat was climbing through her bedroom window the next morning. Boots soaked with morning dew, she thumped onto the dirt-riddled carpet below. The uninvited sun shined into her room, defying the darkness of Kat's decoration theme. Music art posters and magazine tear-outs papered one of the walls—idols she liked the look of, but knew nothing about, judging the messy floors of her room.

Kat pulled the covers from her bed and disarranged the person-shaped pile of pillows underneath. Her mother worked through the night and slept during the day. They only saw each other during the fleeting moments in between and Kat wondered if she even bothered to check her daughter's room when she came home.

Kat sifted through the clothes strewn about her open closet—the clothes she'd been wearing, the clothes she wanted to wear, the clothes she thought others would want her to wear. She settled for something she was supposed to wear. Then she exchanged it for something she probably wasn't.

Tiptoeing down the cluttered hallway, she passed the room of her sleeping mother, who had collapsed into bed, still wearing her waitress uniform. In the kitchen, Kat scarfed down a bag of toaster pops. She had expected to make it back home much earlier, but something about her exhausting first day of school had made her midnight wanderings turn into morning exploration. School and home were both stifling and now she was about to go from one to the other, exhausted and hungry.

As she left the house, Kat discovered her lunch in the folds of her mother's purse, in the form of a handful of dollar bills. She stuffed these in her pocket to join two bottle caps, a broken piece of bike chain, twenty-seven cents, and a pair of scuffed-up sunglasses she had found discarded last night. School would have already started, but it was a short walk.

The bell rang as she slinked through her new favorite side door (she had caught a teacher using it for a secret smoke break yesterday and, sure enough, it was left unlocked today). Classrooms opened and students poured into the hallways, rushing to their next classes. Confused, Kat stood in the middle of the commotion as the students flowed around her.

She grabbed one of the passers-by. "Hey, what period is it?"

"Third period just ended," he said, pulling his arm away.

She had missed her first three classes! Kat wondered if her mother would hear about this. She sauntered to the cafeteria, thinking, *Well, at least I won't be hungry.*

Trying to pretend everything was normal, Kat bought a couple of vending machine snacks for lunch and she scanned the cafeteria as it filled with students. She made her way through the room, lost in thought, as friends met up around her and groups formed at the tables.

In school, she had been taught that stereotyping was bad because any one person in a group isn't going to be exactly like everyone else in the group.

Kat sat in the same place she had yesterday, exhausted and alone. Having things in common with everyone around you didn't seem so wrong. *At least when you are stereotypical, you feel like you belong.*

"I'm telling you, she ain't right." Helen broke Kat out of her reverie when she plopped down across the table from her. "She glares at me when I come through the lunch line."

Cathy sat next to Kat. "She's a little odd, that's all."

"She was talking to the food again!"

"A lot odd?"

Danni arrived in a huff next to Helen.

"Get shot down?" Helen asked, eyes twinkling with ill-hidden amusement.

Danni emptied her lunch bag sullenly. "Sorta."

"Seriously," Helen continued, "you can't let Miss Snotty McSnoddkin's opinions get to you. Who cares what she thinks anyway?"

"Like, everyone?" Danni said. "Everyone cares."

"Snotty McSnoddkins," Cathy sniggered.

Kat spoke up, eyeing Danni's lunch. "I'll trade you some chips for your sandwich."

"You don't have chips," Danni said.

Kat held up her crinkled dollar bills. "I'll get some."

"Why don't you go through the lunch line like me and Cathy?" Helen asked.

"Because," Kat pointed, "*her* sandwich looks good."

"Looks edible," muttered Cathy.

"Hey," said Helen, "At least we've got our appetites back."

CHAPTER FOUR
"A nasty habit"

Kat

As the first days of school became the first weeks, Kat got used to seeing the same faces every lunch period. What she couldn't get used to was that these faces might belong to friends. She had nothing in common with Helen, Cathy, or Danni and it made her nervous to be around them. Soon, they would recognize how different she was and sit somewhere else.

Of course, Helen and Kat were stuck with each other in art class. Today, Kat was scribbling and erasing alternately on a pad of paper. It wasn't part of the assignment. In fact, her piece of poster board lay off to the side, a circle drawn and a slash of yellow paint. They were supposed to be making color wheels, the key to all color awareness, and perhaps even the color universe, the way Mrs. Eggleton explained. So far, Helen had a half-painted, twelve-sectioned circle, and Kat had yet to be impressed.

"You can even create emotion, feelings of warmth and cold…" the teacher was saying.

Kat felt bored. Room temperature, and bored.

Helen's colors were between the lines. Her designs were creative and within Mrs. Eggleton's specifications. Listening to Helen talk, Kat would never have guessed she was in classes with Cathy. Cathy had the word "nerd" written all over her, from her glasses to her awkward conversations, but Helen didn't act like a nerd. Kat couldn't understand how two people who were so different could be friends.

Kat put her fist up to her mouth and began absently chewing on her thumbnail. This assignment didn't interest her, but Kat had laid off the dramatics with Mrs. Eggleton because her class was the only one Kat thought she might enjoy.

She would have to finish the color wheel later, though. She was in the middle of something much more important— drawing comics instead of doing her classwork.

Kat progressed to chewing another finger.

"That's a nasty habit." Helen whispered so Mrs. Eggleton wouldn't hear.

"Is it?" Kat spat out a piece of nail.

Helen pursed her lips. "I'm a knuckle-cracker myself," she ventured.

Kat stared. "Okay," she replied, dully.

What was Helen trying to accomplish here?

Helen sighed and went back to her painting.

Kat scooped up her doodles and jammed them under the table as Mrs. Eggleton stalked by.

"...and the colors across the wheel from each other are the two most suited to complement each other..." She paused behind Kat and said in a loud voice, "If you do not do your work in my class, I will keep you after school to finish." To everybody, she added, "You have one more day to complete this project. Your color wheels must be done by the end of class tomorrow. Next, we will start a project that combines your knowledge of the color wheel with practical application..."

As the teacher moved on, Kat pulled her papers back onto the desk and continued drawing, more determined than ever. Helen set her brush on her tray and leaned over Kat's doodles to see what could be more important than her class work.

"You like drawing comics?"

"Naw, it's my least favorite thing."

Despite her sarcasm, Kat slipped the papers across the table. Helen sifted through them. The pictures portrayed a turtle gym teacher, a dodo history teacher, and a rodent Priscilla Driscalle. Helen wouldn't recognize the teachers, but the other drawings captured Priscilla perfectly.

"I never realized how much Priscilla looks like a squirrel," Helen commented.

"Obsessing over her tail," Kat explained.

"Is this one supposed to be Danni?"

Kat nodded.

"That's funny. Mean, but funny."

Danni had been portrayed as a flamingo, attempting to pass for a peacock. The comic didn't show whether or not she could succeed. Kat hadn't made up her mind about Danni. She was already imagining what animal Helen reminded her of. Something nosy—an anteater, maybe? Or a parrot who never shut up?

"Why do you make them into animals?"

"Can't draw people."

"I guess no one can catch you making fun of teachers if you're drawing pictures of cats and stuff," Helen added.

"Mrs. Eggleton looks more like a gopher, but I'd rather draw cats," Kat whispered.

Kat's observation was spot on, and Helen sniggered behind her palm as Mrs. Eggleton walked by the table next to them. Kat had started to sketch an obnoxious Helen-parrot when her pencil abruptly stopped writing. She picked it up to check the tip, but nothing was broken. Instead, her nails were so long that the pencil had stopped touching the paper. Kat was a habitual nail-biter. She usually had them chewed down to the quick.

She checked her right hand and the nails there were long and sharp as well. Hadn't she just been biting them?

Helen was watching her again. Maybe the nosy anteater was more fitting.

"What's wrong?" Helen asked.

"Nothing!" Kat snapped.

Her fingertips tingled and Kat flexed and rubbed them together. Her nails thickened and lengthened some more. She dropped her pencil and shoved her hands under the table, but accidently jabbed herself in the leg.

"Ouch!" She sprung up, drawing the attention of the students around her.

"Kat, what's going on?"

Was Helen genuinely concerned?

Sweat dampened Kat's armpits. "Nothing! Mind your own business!"

Kat had no idea what was happening. Her fight or flight response had kicked into overdrive and it screamed, *Flight! Flight like you've never flighted before!* Her nails were visibly huge now.

"But it looks like—" Helen started.

Kat scooped her supplies into her backpack while sputtering, "It's just a fricking magic trick. Ha ha, fooled you. You're so stupid. I gotta go."

Kat bolted from class before Helen or Mrs. Eggleton could say a word.

Helen

Helen reflected on the day's events as she showered that night. Even eight hours later, Kat's little nail trick from art class was bothering her. It was a silly thing to keep thinking about. Helen wanted to get to know Kat better, but Kat wasn't as open and easy to talk to as Danni.

Helen rinsed the shampoo out of her hair—a considerable job when taking its length into account. She squeezed the water through it, from root to end, until she was satisfied the suds were gone.

She was about to lather her soap pouf, when a dizzy spell forced her to steady herself against the wall. Her scalp tingled. Helen ran her hands down her hair once more, ducking her head under the warm water. This time, her fingers did not reach the end.

"What?" she said to herself.

Panic set in as her hair gathered around her toes. The panic made it grow faster. In no time, it was up to her shins, gathering around the drain and filling the bath tub.

"Uhhhh…"

Helen clutched her hair at her neck and squeezed, as if doing so could quell the growth, but the hair was increasing from her scalp, and there was no way to hold it back. The dripping locks spilled over the tub and gathered around the door.

"What's happening to me?" Helen cried.

With the drain blocked, the water had nowhere to go, and it soaked through her hair and out onto the bathmat. Squinting through the shower, Helen stretched for the faucet. She felt her feet lifting beneath her.

"No..." she begged, "no, no, nonononono..."

Her fingertips brushed the handles as she lost her footing. Half diving, half falling, Helen succeeded in grasping them, but she let out a yelp as her hair enveloped her. She managed to get the water turned off in time to hear footsteps running up the stairs.

"Stoppit hair! Stop growing!" she whispered.

"Helen!" her mom called from the steps.

Helen thrashed about to right herself in the sodden mass of red around her. Stretching and straining, she pulled her upper half free of the cobweb-like snare her hair had become. She gained something of a sitting position near the top of the mound as her mom reached the landing by the upstairs bathroom.

"Helen?" Her mom was near the door.

"Don't come in!" Helen shrieked. She thrust her hands out, as if she could hold the door shut from several feet away.

"Why? Are you okay?" The door handle rotated, but the hair piled up at the base was enough resistance that it did not open readily. "Why can't I open this door?"

"I'm fine, Mom!" Helen insisted. "That's a towel. In front of the door. Keeping you from opening it. So don't!"

"What? Why not?"

"You'll let out all the steam and I'll get cold."

Helen grabbed her head, trying to stay calm. At least the tingling had stopped and her hair had finished growing. From where she sat amongst the tangled mass, she was halfway up the wall.

"I heard you yell. What's going on in there?"

"Nothing," Helen sputtered. "It was uh—a bug. But it's gone now. Down the drain."

"Why would a bug go down the drain?"

Helen felt like her nonexistent insect, spiraling.

"I think he couldn't take it anymore. Self-immolating spider." Helen cringed as she listened to herself lie.

"That's not nice, Helen."

"You're right, Mom. That was a bad call." Helen just wanted to be alone so she could think. "Police have ruled it an accidental death. His wife and ten million children can move on with their lives."

Her mom hadn't released the door handle. "Are you sure you're okay?"

"Yeah, Mom. Couldn't be better. But you can expect a call from their spider lawyer."

"Helen!"

"Mom! May I *please* finish my shower?"

Helen's mom stepped away from the door, but added, "You know, you don't have to be ashamed about me seeing you naked, Helen. I'm your mother. There's nothing you've got that I haven't seen before."

Helen observed the bathroom and the red hair that filled it. She whispered to herself, "Wanna bet?"

CHAPTER FIVE
"I hate this game"

Danni

Danni tried her best to ignore her little siblings arguing in the hallway. She picked a set of clothes and held it up, comparing outfits against her slim, lanky form in the mirror next to her closet. Danni had spent her summer accumulating a fashionable new wardrobe for the warmer schooldays at the beginning of the year. She had grown taller over the summer, but had not filled out into a mature young lady the way some other girls had.

Taller, ganglier, thin as a stick, and flat as a board. Hopefully, the clothes she had found would accent her tallness nicely or disguise it artfully. And no stains.

"Let's see...blue shirt? Priscilla wore something like that yesterday, she'll think I copied." Danni switched the clothes she

Megan Cain

had been considering for a pink dress with lace trim. "Hmm, trying too hard, and I'd have to do something with my hair. Wait, is that a bruise on my forehead?"

"Gimee!" little Tiffany broke Danni's concentration.

"Nnnoo-ooh!" screamed Addie.

Danni gave up and reached blindly into the closet. A minute later, she opened the door to the hallway, dressed in high-waisted skinny jeans and a logo-bearing crew-neck tee with the sassy pink flats she had put off wearing until the start of the school year.

Inserting herself between the squabbling siblings, Danni seized the purple toothbrush from their tiny-fingered grasp. They peered up at her, wide-eyed and silent, as she inspected the object.

"This is actually mine," she said. "Yours are in the upstairs bathroom."

She marched her toddling sisters up the stairs, through the living room, and into the kitchen, where her mom was making breakfast for the rest of the family.

"Morning," said the blur of activity that personified itself as her mom.

Mrs. Emerson orchestrated from the middle of the kitchen, bouncing Danni's newest baby brother in one arm and pouring milk into cereal bowls around the crowded kitchen table with the other, carefully shouldering her cellphone.

"Alright, I'll tell him," she said.

Danni's mom met her eyes and thrust her shoulder forward, indicating that she needed help with the phone. Danni slid the device from her mom's cheek and hit "end call."

"Danni, don't forget your new inhaler. I left it next to your lunch on the counter."

"Thanks Mom."

Danni poked her next-oldest sister in the arm, causing her to drop her spoon.

"Hey!"

She picked a piece of fruit from the middle of the table, and stood ready for dispatch. There was too much to do in the morning if her mom didn't have help and, as the oldest, it was basically Danni's job.

"Danni, go wake up Zariah and Mitchel, and make sure your dad's tie is tied right because his boss will be at the presentation today." Before Danni could take a step, her mom added, "Oh, and tell Jamie if he stops crying now, I'll let him wear the red one tomorrow."

"Alright." Danni took a bite out of her apple and traipsed down the hallway.

· · · ·

One loud van ride and two periods later, Danni sat with Helen on the cold floor of the gymnasium, waiting for class to begin.

Danni had yet to make any headway with the group she pined to be a part of, and she stuck with Helen most of the time.

Helen seemed to enjoy herself in gym class, when she wasn't going on long runs—or on Fridays—no girl enjoyed gym class on Fridays. To pass the time, Danni and Helen listened as one of Priscilla's clique sobbed to her friends about some drama involving boys.

"…and then he told me he'd rather be with Stacie because *Stacie* didn't have cooties and I told him cooties were *so* third grade and then his stupid friend John butted in and said girls were dumb anyway and then I told John that's not what he thought last week when he was holding hands with Amber and then *he* said…"

"Wow," Helen had been unusually quiet all morning, but this had snapped her out of it. "It's only, like, three weeks into the school year. You wanna be a part of that?"

"Well, yeah," Danni said. "So much happens to them. Wouldn't it be exciting to always be in the middle of things, with so much going on?"

"From what I've seen on *Redundant Desires*, the answer is no."

"Wait. You watch soap operas?"

"What? Soap operas? Who said soap operas? Nobody in this room." Helen picked at a string on her shorts. "Wouldja look at that…"

Danni rolled her eyes. Her goal was to gain the acceptance of Priscilla Driscalle's social group—"the gaggle," as the others called them. She was on friendly terms with most of them, but to truly gain their acceptance, she needed Priscilla's approval—something very difficult to obtain. Besides, Danni was sure that Priscilla wasn't so awful. Why else would she have such a large group of friends?

"Alright, class, listen up!" said their teacher. "Today's game is dodge ball."

"Not again," Danni said in a moan.

"They do this every Friday, what'd you expect?"

"I hate dodge ball," hissed Danni, in a whisper.

"I know."

"I *really* hate dodge ball."

"So you've said."

"Everyone, get up!" continued Ms. Calhoun. "Girls on this side of the gym, boys on the other."

"That's not fair!" There was a collective moan from the girls in their class.

The boys spread out on half of the gym, while the girls shuffled peevishly onto their side. Ms. Calhoun emptied out a bag full of multicolored foam balls into the middle of the court and blew her whistle.

A hoard of boys rushed forward to claim their weapons. A few of the more determined girls also ran into the fray, but only one of them managed to grab a ball, while another took a point-blank throw to the head. When she got up, she went to the sidelines, pouting. A "whoop" sounded from the enemy. First blood was spilled, and the boys liked it.

Danni and Helen stayed together, close enough to the back of the court to avoid detection, but far enough ahead to be seen "participating."

"IhatethisgameIhatethisgameIhatethisgame…"

Helen agreed. "Yeah, it sucks."

Danni's vision clouded and her hand flew to her temple. Pressure was rising between her left ear and eye. She worried there might have been something wrong, but as it reached its peak, the pressure vanished, and Danni decided to remain silent. It was probably one of those things the body does, but doesn't really mean anything.

"Look." Helen elbowed her in the arm.

Danni observed Priscilla and a few of her friends, bombarded by dodge balls. They complained vocally—but their cheeks were rosy and they giggled with delight.

"How can they enjoy being targeted like that?" Danni asked, the first instance where she pictured a downside to being part of Priscilla's group of friends.

Helen folded her arms. "I thought we were past the 'I hit you because I like you' phase."

A yellow ball rolled to Priscilla's feet and the volley stopped as she bent to pick it up. *If Priscilla uses her softball pitching skills, she might stand a chance*, Danni thought. *Of course, if she throws the ball underhanded, she'll look silly, so she has to weigh the possible embarrassment factor of an underhanded dodgeball throw against the humiliation factor of a boy thwarting any other type of throw…*

Priscilla finished her own calculations and threw the ball in a wide, graceful arc to the outstretched arms of one of the boys near the front. Of course, he caught it. Priscilla stuck out her lower lip in the cute pout she had been developing for her Instacam, and she trotted off to join the rest of her team. On the other side, one of the few boys on the sidelines was allowed to join the game once again.

"That's just wrong," Helen said. "If a boy catches the ball, one out-person goes in. If a girl catches the ball, everyone goes back in. How biased."

"We're still losing."

"Doesn't matter. Let's lose quickly, with dignity."

With Priscilla and the majority of the gaggle on the sidelines, there were even fewer girls, and Danni and Helen became targets. Several poorly aimed balls came their way, one arcing widely overhead. Danni shielded herself as the pressure and dizziness occurred again.

"That was close," she said.

Helen looked up. "Not really."

"Ooh, my head feels fuzzy."

A ball whizzed toward Helen, and she jumped to the side, narrowly dodging it. Another came at Danni. As soon as she saw it, she knew it was going to hit her. She was never fast enough to avoid collision and immediate humiliation. All Danni could do was recoil—drop her chin into her chest like a turtle—but before the ball could hit her, a faint *click* sounded in her ear. Her vision clouded once again, and she crumpled to the floor. The ball meant for her passed harmlessly by. Helen gawped at Danni, who lay on the vinyl, blinking in confusion.

Another dodgeball slammed into Helen's cheek, knocking her head sideways. She clenched her jaw as everyone laughed at her.

"Are you okay?" Helen asked, above her.

"Are you?"

"You got hit," Ms. Calhoun shouted.

"I noticed," Helen muttered through her gritted teeth.

"Go to the sidelines!"

Helen trudged off to join the rest of the girls, leaving Danni to dust herself off, alone on the court. Deserted and defenseless. Now, her classmates would see her get pelted to death by every dodgeball-wielding boy in the gymnasium. She would probably fall down again. To make matters worse, she could get knocked unconscious. Or, what if it hurt and she cried—and everyone saw her cry? With all this embarrassment under one roof, the gymnasium would most definitely explode. Priscilla Driscalle would witness her humiliation. Word would spread throughout the school. Even Cathy, Helen, and Kat would shun her.

The boys raised their arms in preparation, dodge balls ready to fly. One of them charged the halfway mark and let loose a blue foam ball of fury. It spun as it flew, catching on its own air current and curving toward her like an angry pitch. Danni's eyes widened as it came for her head, but there was another *click*, and Danni was once again on the floor, safe from dodge ball danger.

Her enemies plotted their next attack, signaling to one another as they readied their aim. Danni regained her feet and the boys unleashed a torrent of dodge balls. Their frightened target squeaked in alarm and ran away with her arms thrown protectively over her head.

Click. Even backwards, she dodged

Click, click.

Danni fell to the ground yet again, rolled to the side, got up to her knees only to fall and roll again. Each movement saved her from the other team, so stubbornly aiming for her defeat.

Panting, she got to her feet one last time and regarded the rest of her team. The girls were dumbfounded by Danni's ability to dodge this impossible onslaught. She caught sight of Helen, who mouthed the words "*look out*" and pointed toward the other side of the court. Danni spun around.

A giant boy with a hairy lip released a powerful throw in her direction. Danni saw it clearly, headed straight for her. It whistled through the still gymnasium air. It was an imperfect dodge ball, wobbling as it flew, a stringy piece of duct tape trailing behind, where the soft green shell had torn and the foam inside was showing. Which part of her face would it would slam into? Would it sting? She could now see every scar and pock mark on its surface.

Click.

49

As if on a spring, her arm swung upward and she snatched the ball from its flight, stopping it in midair. Her white-knuckled grip crushed into the foam. She remained there with arm outstretched, palming the dodge ball. The rest of her team cheered, rushing back onto the court to congratulate Danni and attempt their vengeance on the boys with inspired determination.

Helen grasped Danni by the shoulders, "What was that?"

Danni lowered her arm and the tattered green ball she held. "I-I don't know. My head feels fuzzy."

"Did you say fuzzy?"

"I don't know, like, dizzy-ish?"

Priscilla Driscalle shoved Helen aside, flanked by her gaggle. "Danni! Right? That catch was amazing!"

Danni's eyes welled up in response. "Wait, really?"

"We could use someone with your skills to play right field on the softball team. Misha sucks at it."

"Hey…" the shortest of the gaggle whined.

Helen interjected, "Danni doesn't like sports—"

Danni shoved the dodge ball at Helen and answered, "Of course! I'd love to!"

"Great," Priscilla produced her expert smile, "practice is right here, after school. I'll tell Coach Calhoun."

As Priscilla and her friends swaggered away, Danni beamed with joy. The school hadn't exploded, her popularity had! The softball team was home not just to Priscilla Driscalle, but to Idelle

Jeffries, Tina Hagleman, and Andrea Sodders! Danni didn't know how she had caught that ball, but she knew she had just hit the jackpot of chic. The popularity fountain overflowed! The key to the city of central school gossip shined! The great codex of fashion and style—

"Danni."

In a stupor, Danni responded to Priscilla's mention of practice, "…'kay."

"Danni!"

She shook off her daze and turned to Helen, "Yeah?"

"Your head still fuzzy?"

"Yeah…"

"Then let's go."

"Why?"

Helen gestured to the court, "You want to play more dodge ball?"

．．．．

As Danni finished explaining the problem to Nurse Beaux-Baxter, she still had her doubts about what had happened. She wasn't sure how to describe the fuzziness, or the clicking sound. She couldn't imagine any reason for a person to lose control of her faculties one second, and get back up again the next.

When she was done, Helen asked, "So, what do you think, Nurse B.B.?"

"Well," Nurse Beaux-Baxter scratched her temple. "That sure is different."

The girls leaned forward, hoping for good news.

"But I have just the thing to fix it."

Danni's spine uncoiled—there was a simple explanation to her problem! Nurse Beaux-Baxter dug into one of her desk drawers.

"Now, hold still, sweetie." She pulled out a Band-Aid and pressed it above Danni's eyebrows. "There you go. All better?"

Danni and Helen didn't move. Danni stared cross-eyed at her forehead.

"Go on back to class, dearies." Nurse Beaux-Baxter made a shooing motion at them. "Go on."

Helen was shaking her head as the two left the nurse's office. "Where do you even find people like that? And—and why do you *hire* them?"

"I heard she's the only one who applied for the job."

"There's got to be a better solution than this," Helen peeled the Band-Aid from Danni's brow.

"Ow, ow, ow!" Danni complained at the fresh adhesive clinging to her skin.

"How weird was it?"

"It was pretty weird."

Helen considered the ceiling for a moment, tapping her chin with a knuckle.

"We should all get together after school."

"All of us? What for?" Danni asked. "Not for my fuzzy head?"

"Maybe if we get together, we can figure it out."

"Even Kat?"

"Yeah, why not?"

"I don't think she likes me."

Helen paused. "Sure she does. Besides, if this stuff is happening to you, too, now..."

"Me, too?"

"There's an activity bus we can take home if we stay. I'll tell Cathy and Kat at lunch. We should all get together, figure this fuzzy head thing out..." she trailed off.

CHAPTER SIX
"A sign of what's to come"

Kat

Kat revealed a secret talent when she used Cathy's student ID to free open the door to room 109.

"How did you learn to do that?" Cathy gripped her ID-turned-lockpick, thumbing its newly damaged edges.

Kat shoved her hands in her pockets. "Practice."

"Okay, but why?" Helen asked.

Kat shrugged. She wasn't going to explain to the others how sometimes, she just wanted to go somewhere she wasn't allowed. "Keep Out" signs felt more like invitations.

The three of them snuck inside the room to wait for Danni without being seen. While students with afterschool activities were allowed to linger around the building, any caught without proper excuses would be in trouble—especially having picked a lock.

Cathy flipped on the lights while the others set their book bags near the door. As Cathy joined them, she asked, "Where's Danni?"

"Softball practice, I guess," Helen answered. "She kinda made the team during gym class today."

"You've got to be kidding." Kat grumbled, to no one in particular.

"She's coming though," Helen added.

Kat plunked herself into a desk with a snort. "Softball team" meant "popular girls," and "popular girls" meant waiting. Always.

To pass the time, Helen re-explained the events leading up to her decision to call the small gathering. Kat thought Helen's story was ridiculous, but Cathy had eaten it up excitedly. Problem solving some random mystery was just the kind of thing that would make a nerd like Cathy feel important. Not that Kat would mind a little problem solving, herself. If figuring out Danni's thing could help Kat with her own, she would stick around to find out.

When Danni found them, she was a little dirt covered, but as happy as could be. She waved as she entered the room, "Greetings, wonderful friends!"

"Took you long enough," was Kat's response.

"Practice just ended," said Danni.

"Practice with Priscilla." Kat mocked her in a high-pitched voice.

"We've only got, like, half an hour now," Helen said, disappointed.

"So, what do we do with it?" Cathy asked.

"We still need to find out what's going on in Danni's head," answered Helen.

"You mean the MVP?"

Danni narrowed her eyes at Kat, as if to say *what's your problem?*

"Aside from brain surgery or an MRI, which isn't really an option," Cathy said, "how are we going to do that?"

Kat picked up a magnifying glass from the teacher's desk. Room 109 belonged to Mrs. Francis. Kat had volunteered it for their purposes, hoping she could leave a tack on a chair or damage something before they left. Mrs. Francis happened to have the magnifying glass as part of a collection consisting of a globe, a quill, and several other "historical" artifacts, placed around the room.

She held out the instrument. "One of you brainiac-nerds investigate."

"That'd be you, Cathy," Helen said.

"You're in honors, too," Cathy didn't hesitate to snatch the magnifying glass from Kat.

"Yeah, but you always get As," Helen replied. "I get Bs n'stuff."

Cathy pulled out a keychain and flipped through it to find a small flashlight she had on one of the rings. "Come here," she said to Danni.

Danni obeyed, but with a slowness that betrayed her doubt.

"Now," Cathy snickered, "lend me your ear."

She waited for the laughter that never came, then cleared her throat as if the failed joke was nothing more than a bit of phlegm. She clicked on the flashlight and moved closer to Danni.

Danni pulled back. "Wait. Why do you need my ear?"

"How else is she gonna see inside your head?" Kat asked, rudely.

"You can't see inside someone's head through their ear," Danni said, matching her tone.

"Doctors look in peoples' ears all the time," Helen said.

"I'm not going deaf! I'm going...crazy." Danni dropped her arms, defeated. "This is stupid."

"Helen, can you get my phone?" Cathy asked. "I looked this up earlier."

Helen obliged, taking a moment to dig through her friend's backpack. "Aha!" She pulled out the phone and read from its screen, sounding out the difficult words.

"Abnormalities of the inner ear can lead to a false sense of motion, unsteadiness, or a sensation of falling. A balance disorder may be caused by viral or bacterial infections in the ear. It could also indicate one of many different conditions, such as vestibular neuritis, Meniere's disease, migrainous vertigo, acoustic neuroma, motion sickness, or paroxysmal positional vertigo."

Danni's eyes were so wide she could have scratched her brain with the lashes.

"So, can I please look in your ear?" Cathy said.

"Okay, yeah."

"Wow, internet doctor much?" Kat muttered.

Cathy brought the flashlight and magnifying glass to the side of Danni's head, determined to give this impossible task a good try. She peered hard into Danni's ear and squinted her eyes. Her forehead wrinkled and she lowered her face even closer. Then Cathy jerked back.

"Whoa. That was unexpected."

"What?" Danni asked. "What happened?"

"I think I can actually see inside your head," Cathy replied.

"But that's—"

"Impossible? Here, hold this." Cathy handed the flashlight to Kat and gripped Danni's head to steady it. "Now, what did it sound like again?"

"Like some kind of clicking," Danni answered. "And every time I heard it, I fell over."

"More light," Cathy said.

"Okay, this *is* dumb," Kat moved the flashlight anyway.

"For cripes sakes!" Helen spoke up, having been quiet for too long. "If you keep this up, you're gonna make her dome explode like an ant on the sidewalk."

Danni gasped.

Cathy grabbed her earlobe. "Quit moving. I see something!"

Danni's entire body tensed up on the chair and Cathy had to steady her once again.

"Quit moving. You said this happened in gym class?"

Danni's head bobbled up and down.

"Quit moving! Helen?"

"Yeah, during dodgeball," Helen answered.

"...Interesting."

Danni wrung her hands. "What is it what is it what is it?!"

"For lack of a better explanation, it looks like...an object." Cathy said.

"An object!" Danni flinched.

"In the shape of...a hexagon."

"A hexagonal object!"

"With words on it."

"A hexagonal object with words on it!" Danni sobbed.

"What could possibly be a worse explanation than that?" Kat snatched the magnifying glass and pushed Cathy aside. She glanced at Danni's ear. "What are you talking about? There's nothing there."

"No!" Cathy pleaded, "Look longer! Really look."

Kat irritably pursed her lips, but she did what Cathy asked. At first, she saw nothing. But as she stared, Danni's ear canal pulled inward, expanding as it did so. Kat's vision was drawn into a vast darkness through the magnifying glass. She leaned in closer, just as Cathy had. There was no way this could be happening. She didn't see any earwax, or a big squishy brain, or anything realistic that should be inside a person's head—only a large void and flashes of brilliant color—thoughts perhaps—dancing within. Something began to take form.

Kat's jaw dropped open and she muttered, "Uh, it's a sign."

"A sign of what's to come?" Danni asked.

"No, like a *sign*, sign."

"Am I gonna die?" whispered Danni.

"It says," Kat squinted to read, "'DUCK.'"

"Oh, no, I *am* gonna die!"

"Quit moving!" Kat and Cathy yelled in unison.

Danni grabbed the sides of her face in terror, knocking the magnifying glass from Kat's grip in the process. The flying object arced through the air and as its shadow passed over Danni, a subtle *click* sounded in the silence of the room. Danni's arms shielded her fragile head and she collapsed on the floor in the duck and cover position. The magnifying glass clunked on the tile next to her.

"Was that it?" Kat asked.

"Do it again!" Cathy said as Danni got back to her feet.

Kat was happy to assist. She lobbed the small flashlight at Danni's back. A faint *click* once again, and Danni's face hit the carpet. The jangling keychain sailed harmlessly above her and smacked into the white board.

Danni jumped to her feet. "What's going on?"

Cathy tossed a pencil and again Danni fell, with a *click* and increasing predictability.

"I don't like this!" Danni got up.

A book flew at her.

Click.

Danni fell down. She got back to her feet.

This time, an eraser.

Click. Danni collapsed.

"Stoppit!" She stood. "That one was too close!"

A paper airplane.

Click—

Danni's hand shot up to catch and crush the floating paper.

"I mean it!" she yelled. "Oh, wait a minute. What just happened?"

Cathy retrieved the now cracked magnifying lens and flashlight. She studied Danni's ear and turned to Helen with a puzzled expression.

"It says, 'CATCH.'"

Helen, who had been watching the scene with curled lips, cackled with glee.

"What's wrong with me?" Danni said, dropping the plane.

"You've got a duck-o-meter in your head!" Helen squealed. "*In your head!*"

"Of course," Cathy said. "Each time something is thrown at you, it clicks to the next side and after five 'DUCKs', you get a 'CATCH.'"

Helen covered her mouth and chortled.

"It's not funny!" Danni whined.

"Yes it is. It's hilarious," said Helen.

Kat had found it less amusing by the second. She could throw things at Danni's head all day, but something about the tall girl's complete lack of control over her body was too disturbingly familiar to Kat. This so-called search for answers had left her more confused than before. Her fingertips were tingling.

"It makes sense," explained Cathy. "Your absolute hatred of dodge ball has manifested itself in the form of this 'duck-o-meter' in your brain—mental to physical."

"Makes sense?" Kat said. No one had noticed her increase-ing discomfort. "You talk about this stuff like it happens to people every day! You use big words, like *man-i-fest*, but none of this is normal. None of what's been happening to us is frick-ing normal!"

As she spoke, her fingernails grew longer and harder. The bases grew denser, and when she slammed her palm on a nearby desk in frustration, she cut clean through the metal sidebar. Kat raised her hand to her face. No injuries, but her nails had spread back to cover her fingers, creating sharp points and knife-like edges. Kat took a very deep breath, trying to calm the churning nerves in the pit of her stomach. Slowly, her shaky hands faded back to normal. The commotion over Danni's head had been forgotten.

"The changes are getting more powerful," she whispered. Kat picked up her backpack and headed for the door. "And I'm scared," she said to herself.

CHAPTER SEVEN
"Okay...so it grows."

Cathy

Cathy, Helen, and Danni remained silent, stunned by the extent of Kat's transformation and respecting her temper. Once she had left, Helen got up to analyze the damaged desk.

"If we keep messing up school property, we're gonna get in trouble," she said, singing the word "trouble."

"That's the least of our problems," answered Danni.

"Right," Helen said. "So, we'll list the strange things that have happened to us. Maybe we can figure out where this thing is going."

"Or where it's been," Cathy jumped in. She brought a notebook and pencil from the teacher's desk. "If we learn when it happened, or what started it, we can learn how to reverse it."

"Okay," Danni said, "so, what's happened? There's this thing in my head—"

"The duck-o-meter," Helen finished.

Danni flashed her a side eye. "We're not calling it that."

"And it's obvious what's happening to Kat." added Cathy.

"What were you telling me this morning?" Helen asked Cathy. "Before class?"

"Oh," Cathy said. "It's not any one thing in particular. It's, well...I finished washing a week's worth of dishes in thirty minutes last night."

"That's okay," Danni said.

"I broke most of them."

"Oh."

"On Monday, I did all the homework we had for the entire week."

"Jeez," said Helen, "you *are* a brainiac-nerd."

"I got everything wrong!" Cathy said. "I didn't even read the questions!"

"It's odd," Helen slid into a desk and scooched it around to face them. "But I'm not sure it's what we're looking for. Was there more?"

"Yeah, that same night, I couldn't sleep, so I made up stuff."

"Made up stuff?" Danni asked.

"Yeah. Like homework assignments for the rest of the year. And stuff I needed to move around the house. My parents weren't happy about that one. They couldn't understand why I put my tita's meatball recipe on the fridge, or why the T.V. was facing the back porch. Like, was I hungry? Am I sick of the news? I rearranged my room. I ruined one of my sister's paintings. It was compulsive, but it made sense at the time." Cathy's expression glazed over while she recounted the memories. "This morning, I drank a bottle of syrup for breakfast and ran to school."

"Bottle of syrup?" Danni scrunched up her nose, disgusted.

"Ran to school?" Helen was shocked. "How many miles is that? Aren't you tired?"

Cathy felt her eye twitch. "I got to class early, collapsed on the floor for five minutes, and woke up fine."

"So that's why the side of your face was red."

"Wait a minute," Danni said. "Did you get dressed in this condition?"

"Uh, yeah?" Cathy dropped her chin, inspecting.

"Ohthankgoodness!" Danni exhaled all at once. "I thought you wore that on purpose. I didn't wanna say anything."

"You thought I put my shirt on backward on purpose?" Cathy exclaimed.

Danni evaluated Cathy's disheveled clothing again, "This qualifies."

"Anything else?" Helen asked.

Cathy shook her head as she pulled her arms in to fix her shirt.

Danni lifted a hesitant hand, "I may have something else."

"Okay, go."

Danni began, "I woke up last night, and I had to pee—"

"Oh, that's the epitome of strange."

"Shut up, Helen. Do you want to hear it or not?"

"Hear about you peeing? No thanks."

Danni shouted to keep Helen from interrupting. "I woke up to pee! I got out of bed! And I think I hit my head on the top of the door frame!"

The room was silent and uncomfortable once her voice faded.

"I don't know if that counts," Danni added quietly.

Helen smiled and bit her lip.

Danni slumped in her chair. "Just say it."

"Obviously the duck-o-meter wasn't working yet."

"Real funny, Helen."

"You have to be at least seven feet tall to bump your head like that," Cathy said.

"I thought I was just tired." Danni shrugged. "I felt fine this morning."

"What about you, Helen?" Cathy asked.

"Me?"

"Has anything happened to you?"

"Uh, nope." Helen's hesitation was not convincing.

"Nothing?"

"Nuthin'."

"What about your hair?"

"What *about* my hair?"

"It used to stop below your waist," Cathy explained.

"Aaand?"

"And now it's below your butt."

"So, you mean to tell me," Helen's hazel eyes sparked. "That you've been looking at my butt."

"C'mon Helen," Danni begged for seriousness.

"So, it's a little long. I like it long—oh no."

Woosh!

Cathy and Danni staggered as a shock wave tore through the room. Every desk shifted, their legs groaning against the floor in protest. Objects blew off the walls and the teacher's ancient overhead projector toppled from its cart. There had been no giant flash of light to blind them, no magical music-filled ascent to transformation, but one second the room was empty, and the next, it was filled with Helen's hair.

"Okay," Helen sighed. "So, it grows."

"Grows!" Danni exclaimed. "It grows? That's an under-statement!"

"Floods is more accurate," added Cathy.

Tangled waves of red flowed behind Helen, wove through the desks, and poured across the tile. Uncountable strands carpeted the floor—some frizzy, some wavy, some straight, and some curly. To top this off, it glowed. There was something about it that dizzied the senses and confused reality.

"Helen," breathed Danni. "It's horrible."

"It's not so bad."

"Did you know about this?" Cathy asked.

"Maybe."

"Can you move?"

"Uh…" Helen shifted her weight and strained her neck, but made no progress at dislodging herself from the desk. "No."

Danni picked up a fallen clock that lay cracked on the floor. "It's almost time to go. You'll miss the bus if we don't get out of here soon."

"You guys go ahead," said Helen. "I kinda like it here."

"Nonsense." Danni leered. "Cathy, why don't you go find me some scissors."

Helen's eyes followed Cathy as she dug around in the teacher's desk.

"That's not funny, Danni. Can we, uh, can we call a truce on the funny?"

Danni held out her hand and Cathy handed her the pair she had found. "Sure."

"That doesn't look like a truce on the funny," said Helen.

Danni turned up her palms. "We have to get you out of here somehow."

Writhing in her seat, Helen cried, "Don't! Please! I-I never cut my hair!"

"Well, you can't stay there," Cathy reasoned.

"Oh, yes I can, traitor!"

"It's called tough love." Danni snippy-snipped her instrument of destruction.

"Wait! Just give me a minute!" Helen struggled. "Go away!"

Danni reached for the hair, but Helen slapped her hand.

"Fine. I'll start from the outside and work my way in."

Helen growled, "I thought you were my friend!"

Danni wasn't listening, convinced she was doing the right thing. Cathy wanted to take Helen's side, but she agreed that cutting her away from her hair was the most logical solution. She fought the impulse to intervene for her friend as Danni inched closer.

Florescent light shined on the scissors and Helen cringed. Throughout the room, the hair shook once, as if zapped by lightning, like Doctor Frankenstein's monster.

Danni, intent on the task at hand, was more than a little taken aback when two long tufts of hair rose from the red mass to defend it.

"It's alive!"

The tufts of hair came at Danni and she screamed, swinging the scissors to defend herself. One of them wrapped around her thrashing wrist and Danni froze. The other wrenched the scissors from her hand and flung them away. The sharp metal whizzed past Cathy's ear and lodged itself in the whiteboard. After an uneasy stillness, Helen's hair relaxed and she was able to stand.

"Why didn't you tell us?" Cathy asked.

"I didn't know it could do that." Helen swiveled her head toward Danni and the hair released her. "Whenever I think too much about it, this happens—it grows. That's why I didn't say anything. I filled the shower last night and the bedroom this morning. When I concentrate on how much I need it to go away, it goes away." As though on command, the hair began to recede. "I'm going home now."

"Helen..."

She ignored Danni and gave Cathy a final disappointed glance as she picked up her backpack and dragged what was left of her diminishing hair out the classroom door.

Cathy surveyed what was left of the room. Most of the desks were now toppled and nothing else remained in its original place. Broken acrylic from the fallen projector crunched beneath Cathy's feet.

"That's not good."

"Is Helen okay?"

"Um, no. She has sort of a thing about her hair."

"Obviously."

"It's a pretty big thing." Cathy tiptoed out of the mess. "Anyway, we gotta go before anyone sees this."

"Right."

Danni peeked outside to make sure the coast was clear. The last thing they needed was to get blamed for the mess inside, even though it was completely their fault.

As they snuck through the school, she told Cathy, "I called my mom to tell her about softball practice, so she's going to pick me up. I can ask her to give you a ride, too."

Cathy stopped in her tracks. "That's nice of you."

"Look," Danni said, "I have, like, a million siblings, and I love being in the middle of a big family. If I'm popular, I can have a million friends, too, and that includes you guys."

"I guess that makes sense."

"Yeah, I like hanging out with you. So, about the ride?"

Cathy weighed her options. "I've never seen Helen that mad. It might be weird to ride the bus with her—are you sure it's okay?"

Danni smiled. "Yeah!"

"Then Helen can have the weekend to calm down."

"Mm-hm." Danni nodded.

As they walked to the exit, Cathy told Danni about Helen's hair. "We met in grade school last year, and believe it or not, she was the shy one in class, being the new kid. Most of us had been together since first grade, so it took a while for her to get into the group. She's funny, so that helped, but her hair is what made her stand out."

"Of course."

"Anyway, for fifth grade graduation, her mom took her to a salon and they trimmed it too much. Helen flipped out. She even cried. No one else noticed. No one would care, except she thinks her hair defines her—that she's not her without it."

"So, you're telling me her hair is short right now?" Danni asked with disbelief.

"Not anymore. That's for sure."

"Yeah. But I suppose we'd look at her differently if she was bald," mused Danni. "Maybe that explains her hair problems, kind of like my duck—um, this thing inside my head."

"Yeah, but it doesn't explain mine."

"I guess not."

Cathy pulled her wallet from her backpack. "I'm going to get a quick snack from the vending machine."

She was relieved when Danni didn't give her craving a second thought, but that relief disappeared when she turned the corner. The snack machine had been destroyed. The shattered safety glass glinted under the florescent lights and the contents lay spilled across the floor. Cheesy crunches popped under their feet as Cathy and Danni moved in to investigate.

"All the candy bars and cake snacks are gone," Cathy said, disappointed.

"But most of the chips are still here," Danni pointed out. "Somebody had a real sweet tooth."

"What should we do?" Cathy asked.

"I don't want anything to do with this—" Danni said.

"Shouldn't we tell some—"

"—because I don't want to get in trouble for that." She thumbed in the direction of classroom 109.

"Oh."

"Let's get out of here."

"Just a minute." Cathy selected a bag of trail mix from the broken machine. "I guess this will do." She dropped a few quarters into the mess. She wasn't a thief, after all.

As they hurried outside, Danni whispered, "I bet Kat did that."

"I don't think she would."

"You don't think she'd steal?"

"I'm not sure about that, but she wouldn't have to break it open if she can pick a lock."

"She was pretty mad. Maybe she just wanted to break something…"

CHAPTER EIGHT
"In a calm and orderly fashion"

Cathy

Cathy tapped her pencil on the side of the chair. Her homework sat blank on the desk before her in the room she shared with Lucy. She should have been done with it by now, but she had been finding it difficult to focus lately. She was supposed to be answering questions about the history chapter she had read on Marie Antoinette, but all she could think about was how many airplanes were flying in the storm outside. Seven-forty-sevens doing loop-de-loops in the rain.

A loud noise snapped her back to attention—Lenny's TV. It wasn't fair he got a TV in his room—or his own room, for that matter. Cathy shifted to her homework and began filling in the answers.

"Let them eat custard…" she mumbled.

Her eyes drifted back to the window and the rain drops falling against the glass. Lenny was watching a cartoon show that was so loud and obnoxious she could practically see the flashing colors with her ears. The clock on the wall ticked louder. The wind blew branches against the side of the house. Her dad opened a can of soda in the kitchen. A floorboard creaked. The rain trickled. Lenny picked his nose.

Thunder clapped, and Cathy was on her feet. Her mind went blank, and she wandered out into the hallway, a robot with a secret directive. She paced from room to room, collecting items—glue, tape, and twine. She grabbed a rubber ducky and a frizzy hairbrush from the bathroom. Three forks and a spoon and a bag of toasty pops from the kitchen. She acquired clay and paint from her sister's art supplies.

Her brother was still glued to the screen as she crept into his room to snatch a couple of toys. Cathy made several trips to and from the basement for her collection. She finished up with some clothes and a bucket from the laundry room and knelt on the floor, surrounded by her supplies.

Supplies for what? she questioned, fighting for clarity. *What am I doing?*

Her hands were already moving. Wrapping items, tangling them, gluing them together. Faster and faster and faster she moved. Her hands were a blur. The room was a blur. Her thoughts were a—

She pulled on the twine, and the monstrosity rose into the air and fitted itself against the ceiling, a giant disk of random junk. Cathy craned her neck back until she plopped down underneath her creation.

"What did I just do?"

"Wow!"

The commotion had drawn Cathy's family downstairs as she finished her contraption.

"That sure is...something." her dad scratched his balding head. "Whatcha got there, Cathy-Bear?"

"It's, u-uh..." Cathy stammered.

"My Power Guy action figure!" Lenny cried, pointing. "And those are pieces of my Sir Spuddy Skull!"

"My hair brush...the pizza cutter..." listed her mom.

"You're a rotten thief!" Lenny shouted. "Gimme my stuff back!"

Cathy was in a daze. She had no idea what had happened, let alone how to explain it to her family. As if on cue, her mom asked:

"Catalina, can you explain this?"

"I—"

"Why didn't you tell us you were into at 3-D art?" Lucy exclaimed. "It's amazing!"

"3-D art?" Cathy and her mom asked in tandem.

"This is much better than what you did to my painting. I'm a little jealous."

"Jealous?" Cathy pointed to herself. "Of me? What are you talking about?"

Her family admired the piece from below and Cathy wondered if she hadn't entered a parallel dimension.

Lucy tiptoed around the composition, studying it. "You've perfectly captured the inner turmoil of a materialistic society. The way the viewer feels like it could collapse on top of them at any moment, crushing them under a pile of wasted dreams."

"Maybe Lucía should come out from underneath it," their mom said, reaching for her daughter. "Maybe we should all take a step back."

"What about my toys?" Lenny insisted.

"You never play with those anyway," Lucy said. "Let her keep them for a while."

"I suppose it's not hurting anything here in the basement." Cathy's mom eyeballed the sculpture. "At least until we make another pizza. Come on, kids. You should be in bed by now. Vámonos!"

"Aw, but it's the weekend!"

"You heard your mother. Vamoose!"

Her sister congratulated her once again, and Cathy continued to analyze her inexplicable creation as the rest of her family marched up the stairs. She wished she could be proud of herself, but talent had nothing to do it. It was this thing that was happening to her and her friends. Cathy could only imagine what they would find if they looked inside *her* ear right now. She was about to go upstairs with the rest of her family, when something within the cluster caught her attention. Cathy's heart sank.

Her homework.

Danni

Danni clutched her book bag straps and marched into the school. It was a little early in the season for the weather to be getting so cool, but it provided the opportunity for her to sport cute sweaters and maybe a light jacket that she could shop for next weekend. Perfect for her induction to Priscilla Driscalle's circle.

Danni pushed open the doors and shivered off the cold as she passed between them. A cluster of girls talked amongst themselves to her left. She could separate them easily from the rest of the crowd because, as they gathered in the center of the common area, everyone else revolved around them.

One of the girls waved. Danni peeked around and realized the wave had been meant for her. She waved back, delighted. One softball practice, and she was in! Last Friday, her performance had been questionable. She couldn't do much without clothes to change into, but just being there was enough to begin new friendships. Danni headed towards the girls but stopped as someone brushed by her from behind.

"Sorry," Helen muttered. She kept walking.

Danni wavered. Surely, a hesitation wouldn't cost her too dearly. She called for Helen to wait up and jogged over to her. Helen frowned at the floor, refusing to make eye contact.

"Are you still mad?" Danni asked, even though she knew the answer.

Helen shrugged.

"Hey, I'm sorry."

Now, Helen looked at her.

"I got carried away. You were being so annoying with all the joking. I didn't know it was a big deal. I mean, I help with my sisters' hair and when it needs cut, we cut it. I didn't know it was so important to you. Cathy told me."

"Yeah, well, I guess you were trying to help."

Danni smiled. "You were pretty stuck."

Helen smiled back. "Yeah, I was."

"Were you planning to stay mad?"

Helen scrunched her mouth sideways as she considered. "Dunno. Not forever. Maybe a week."

"Who would I talk to in gym class?"

Helen head-gestured to Priscilla.

"Oh. Then who would you talk to?"

"Myself," came the reply. "I'm great company."

"Heh, only sometimes," Danni said.

"Anyhoo," Helen de-slouched and hiked up her backpack. "I'll see you in gym. I've gotta hurry to class and finish my homework."

"How do you get such good grades if you don't do your homework?"

"I do it. Just not right away."

. . . .

During the morning announcements, the principal menaced the whole school over Friday's sudden rash of vandalism. Cathy and Helen buried their noses in their math books.

. . . .

"...An investigation is under way, and I assure you the perpetrator or *perpetrators* of these heinous acts will be found..."

Danni slouched in her seat.

. . . .

"...If anyone knows anything about the vandalism, I encourage you to come forward..."

Kat doodled on her desk, smirking.

"...and I expect these exploits to stop, and that the remainder of the school year will continue in a calm and orderly fashion."

CHAPTER NINE

"Think small"

Helen

Danni had spoken to her that morning, so when she didn't show up by attendance call for gym class, Helen knew something was wrong. And, given their situation, whatever was wrong could also be unexplainable, uncontrollable, or horrifying. She raised her hand to make an excuse for Danni.

"Um, she's sick, Ms. Calhoun."

One of the gaggle interrupted with "No she's not. I saw her in the bathroom."

"Will somebody go check on her?" Ms. Calhoun had asked.

Before anyone else could volunteer, Helen claimed the job for herself and dashed to the locker room, calling for Danni once she was inside.

"Helen?" Danni's voice was raspy. "Thank goodness it's you."

Helen had walked into a post-disaster, demolished bathroom. Paper towels littered the floor. A burst pipe sprayed water through a crack in the wall. The florescent light flickered on the ceiling, and the last of the three stalls had imploded slightly. There was sobbing from within.

"I'm not coming out!"

"Danni, whatever it is, I'm sure it's not that bad." Helen waited, tapping her foot.

"I'm staying here until it goes away."

"Until what goes away?" Helen asked. "You better not be getting us both in trouble over a zit!"

"A zit!" Danni cried. "Do I have a zit, too? Why didn't you tell me? I wanna die!"

"For cripes sakes," Helen snapped, "you don't have a zit! Now, what's going on?"

Danni said, "You remember when we were talking about the stuff that's been happening to us?"

"Of course, I remember."

"Well…"

The stall door latch clacked. It creaked open on its damaged hinges and a five-foot-long leg slid out from inside. It was followed by the rest of Danni, immense and stretched out of proportion. Danni's blue gym shorts fit like bikini bottoms and she had folded her exceptional arms across her chest to keep the uniform shirt stretched down modestly. Kneeling on the floor, she swayed back and forth to keep her impossible form balanced. Her neck was two feet long. Her hair brushed against the ceiling. With an equally elongated face, she stared at Helen.

"Is it terrible?" came a small voice.

"I..." Helen blinked hard and rubbed her eyes with disbelief. "I...um..."

"I don't know how it happened." Tears were making the long trek down Danni's formidable chin. "I put on my gym uniform, and I was putting on lip gloss in the mirror when I saw how—you'll think it's dumb."

"Danni..."

"How long these stupid shorts made my legs look."

"Oh."

"My skin was tingling, so I went into this stall and..."

"What happened to my hair happened to you," Helen finished.

Danni nodded, shaking loose a couple more tears. "Why does only your hair get longer, when it happens to my entire body?"

"I don't think it's about getting longer."

Danni sniffed.

"My hair is kinda important to me," Helen explained. "And, I guess if your image is important to you, in a twisted sort of way..."

"There's more of me..."

"Yeah."

"To be self-conscious about?"

"Yeah. It's only a theory, though."

"That's not fair." Danni wiped her nose. "So, what do I do?"

Ms. Calhoun's voice yelled at them from the locker room entrance. "Hughes! Emerson! If you don't come out here and join the class, I am writing you both detentions!"

"What do I do? What do I do?" Danni panicked.

"I'll go out there and buy you some time. Just fix it."

"How?"

"I don't know," Helen said as she ran off. "Think small."

Danni

With that, Helen was gone, and Danni was alone once again. Her, and a wall-length bathroom mirror.

"Think small. Think small," whispered Danni. "Thinking small…"

Danni pictured mice and bees and Marbie Dolls, but nothing happened. Tears were threatening to break loose again. Her embarrassment hadn't made the school explode, but it had destroyed the bathroom.

As she scanned the area around her, she was horrified at the thought of what her reflection might show, but morbid curiosity compelled her to look. At a crouch, Danni crept to the mirror.

An alien form appeared in the glass and she leaned closer to inspect it with disbelieving eyes. She touched her cheek. The image in the mirror, with its eight-inch-long fingers, followed her movements precisely.

Like Helen's mutated hair, there was a peculiar brightness to her—something unreal, impossible, but somehow still existing. Shouldn't she be in pain? Shouldn't her body crumple to have its insides stretched so? She saw herself, so huge in comparison to her surroundings and a thought occurred to her that might help her to reform.

Danni closed her eyes and visualized herself as she should be, proportioned to the things around her, able to stand on the tips of her toes and reach upward with space to spare. Her skin tingled. A familiar fuzziness overtook her mind, but Danni continued to imagine being shorter than her dad, her feet still far from the edge of her bed, and ultimately, being able to fit into her stupid gym uniform.

The fuzziness faded and she opened her eyes to see her body had reverted back to its normal, lanky shape. Danni lifted her hands to her face once again. It dizzied her mind to know that, seconds ago, they had been big enough to surround her head. Danni exhaled slowly, calming herself. With a paper towel, she blotted the wetness from her cheeks and chin. One last glance, to make sure everything was truly alright, and she jogged out into the gymnasium, where Helen was waiting with a basketball.

"You okay?" she asked.

"I think so," Danni said. "How's my hair?"

"It looks like it got caught in a ceiling fan."

Danni winced and Helen handed her the ball.

"We're practicing free throws."

Danni took the ball, but did nothing. "What are we gonna do?"

"I don't know," Helen said, with a sincere pinch of her lips, "but I'll think of something."

Helen

Helen put her brain to work through the rest of class and into the following lunch period. There was only one solution to their problem, something she had been mulling over since their first meeting, but convincing the others to see things her way would be difficult.

"So how about the announcement they made this morning?" Cathy asked as the girls sat at lunch together.

"They don't know a dang thing," Kat said. "They're just trying to scare us into turning ourselves in."

"What about the vending machine?" Danni added, targeting the question at Kat.

"What vending machine?" Helen asked.

Cathy and Danni related what they had come upon to Helen and Kat.

"That'll put you in a tight spot, Danni. Now you've been at three sites of vandalism."

"Three?" asked Kat, a devious and approving smirk in Danni's direction.

"Oh, yeah," Helen continued, "Danni grew ten feet tall today. It was disturbing—but cool. Destroyed the girls' locker room, though."

"Just the bathroom," Danni muttered. "I told Coach Calhoun it wasn't like that when I left."

"It wasn't like that when you left?" Kat asked. "They really bought that?"

"What? Like an ordinary kid can explode a bathroom? They think it was sewer gas or something," Helen said. She put her hand to her chest, feigning astonishment. "And it was a miracle no one was in there when it happened!"

"We have to do something about this," Danni sulked.

"Oh yeah? Like what?" Kat said.

"Well, first," Helen took over, "who else has had an accident since Friday?"

Cathy and Danni raised their hands. Helen followed suit. They watched Kat expectantly.

"Okay, put your arms down. I had kind of a nightmare last night, and when I woke up, my sheets were shredded."

"You sure you didn't turn into a werewolf?" Danni said under her breath.

Kat narrowed her eyes at Danni. "Funny."

"But how do we stop all of this? Cathy asked. "What should we do?"

Helen leaned in to the center of their table. "We should practice."

"What?" Danni said.

Cathy's voice was small. "I'm not sure that's a good idea."

"You want to *make* these things happen?" Danni said. "That's insane!"

"I don't know," Kat spoke up. "She might be right."

Danni's mouth dropped open.

"If we can't stop this from happening, maybe we should learn to control it," reasoned Kat.

"Exactly," Helen said, snapping her fingers to point at Kat. "I want it to go away as much as anyone, but we don't even know what started it. The school nurse is nuts, and a real doctor wouldn't believe us. Even then, we couldn't prove what was going on to any doctor unless we knew how to safely produce it. Which we don't."

The table was silent as Helen laid out their predicament.

"I'd rather cure it."

"But we've got nothing, Danni."

"We've got the potatoes," said Cathy.

"The potatoes? That's absurd," Helen said. "Excuse me, mister doctor, sir? I ate some mashed potatoes and now my hair won't stop growing. No just me, and not the *whole school* that also ate them." Cathy hung her head and Helen continued. "We should practice a couple times a week after school. We can work out the when and where at lunch, when we're all together."

Kat agreed, a brief dip of her chin.

"Yeah, I guess," Danni said.

They waited for Cathy's response.

"O-okay. If everyone else thinks so."

"Perfect," Helen said. "Now, let's come up with somewhere else to do this, so we don't keep damaging the school. It's a miracle we haven't gotten caught with everything that's already happened…"

CHAPTER TEN
"Enough excitement for the night"

Helen

Helen, Cathy, Kat, and Danni made a circle, sitting cross-legged near the tree line, out of sight. Helen had offered up her house first. It had a large backyard and the property met the edge of a forested county park, so they would have plenty of privacy. The four of them had done nothing but talk nervously at first, but the chatter had since given way to apprehensive silence. Dusk crept across the sky as they waited for something to happen.

Kat spoke up. "This is getting us nowhere."

"I suppose 'practice' means we should actually do something," Helen joked.

"Should we go one at a time, or all together?" Danni asked.

"I dunno," Helen mulled over the question. "I suppose it'd be easier on us if we tried it together—you know, so we don't have the pressure of everyone watching us,"

"Yeah, but if one of us needs help, the rest of us probably will, too," Kat said. "Then where will we be?"

"Good point."

"S-so who goes?" Cathy asked.

"Danni and I have had practice forcing ourselves to get normal again, so maybe it should be one of us." Helen said.

"Be my guest," Danni replied.

"But neither of us knows how to make it happen."

"It always happens when I don't want it to," Kat said.

"Yeah, like in gym class," Danni added. "Or when Helen's trying to pretend it doesn't happen at all."

Helen wrinkled her brow. "So, we should focus on keeping it from happening to make it happen? It's worth a shot."

"So, go ahead," Kat goaded.

Helen took a deep, nervous breath and concentrated. She closed her eyes and pictured all the awful trouble she had experienced since her hair started transforming. She dug up each memory and thought to herself, *now don't do* that*! It sure would be horrible if* that *happened again*…

Helen exhaled. "Nothing."

Across from her, Cathy stared at the ground, shaking and twitching.

"Cathy? Are you okay?" Helen asked.

"Soup."

"What?"

"Can't think."

"Do you need to—"

"Gonna explode."

The others jumped back.

"Bonsai."

A shockwave knocked the girls onto their backs. When they clambered to their feet, they were stunned to see Cathy sitting in the middle of a spherical grassless dip in the ground. She continued twitching. The bright aura surrounding her was much more apparent in the waning sunlight. Cathy's glasses were cockeyed and her hair stuck out in frizzy strands. Her clothes were disheveled, her shoelaces untied.

"Cathy?"

"French poodle."

"Are you alright?" Helen took a tentative step into the ditch.

"*French poodle.*"

Helen checked with Danni and Kat before replying. "Cathy, we don't understand."

"We!" Cathy's pupils were dilated, deep black. "We, we, oui! We are a group. I am talking to a group. A group of oui. Oui is 'yes' in French. French poodles come from, *duh*, France. Therefore, French poodle means 'yaaas.'"

Helen's face was slack-jawed, unsure of how to respond.

"Haven't you ever seen a—" Cathy twitched "—t-t-train of logic?"

"So, you're alright?" Kat asked, skeptical.

"No! Do I look alright to you? What's happening to me?"

Cathy's desperate brown eyes shot from one person to the next, settling on Helen. Her pupils re-dilated.

"Gotta run."

She was gone.

Faster than someone could say, "Cathy, let's take you to a hospital," she had covered more distance than the world's greatest athletes could have dreamed. She tore across the grass and hurdled over the bushes on the edge of Helen's yard, leaving her friends behind her.

Helen shook herself from her stupor. "We have to help her!"

Another shockwave sent dirt flying at Kat and Danni.

Helen's figure glowed faintly as she followed Cathy's exceptional trail, but the end of her hair stayed put, lengthening as she ran ahead. Kat and Danni glanced at each other, then gave chase, one on each side of Helen's flowing red tresses. The hair stopped growing and took up the rear of their procession, dragging lightly over the greenery.

Cathy lurched to avoid a rocky outcrop and darted back and forth amongst the trees. She was not in control of herself, and it was a matter of time before she got hurt.

"Cathy!" Helen yelled. "Stop!"

"Can't stop!" Cathy shouted in return. "Legs too fast!"

Cathy veered straight for the trunk of a large tree. If she couldn't stop, she was going to run into it. Danni and Kat were nearly there, but none of them could do anything if they didn't think fast. She had to be stopped, or if she hit the tree, she needed...

"Padding!" Helen screamed.

She willed her hair forward, while still running to intercept her friend. The hair balled and collected itself between Cathy and the tree, forming a kind of pillow in her path. The crazed Cathy hurled into the giant pillow with all her force, yanking Helen off her feet. When Kat and Danni caught up, they witnessed Helen, Cathy, and Helen's massive ball of hair slam into the old tree trunk, which let out a hollow *crack*.

"Are you guys okay?" cried Danni.

There was another thunderous *crack*, followed by many more as the trunk splintered. Small branches rained from overhead. With a moan, the old hollow trunk swayed above them.

"It's gonna fall!" Kat yelled.

Helen and Cathy were tangled together in the pile of hair, unable to free themselves. Kat and Danni rushed in to help them.

A large branch snapped. Kat ducked to the side, narrowly avoiding its crash into the dirt. The mass of red hair entwined itself around her ankles. Danni was frantic, digging through the hair to find Cathy, who had still not surfaced.

"Helen! Get control of your hair," she cried.

Helen's scalp stung. Her neck ached. She was too disoriented to know what her hair was up to now.

The old oak creaked and groaned as it gave way, showering the four girls with more snapping twigs and branches. It was coming down on top of them. Helen filled with horror as its shadow fell over her. She was about to die.

Danni

A third shockwave, and Danni had doubled in size. Tripled. Her brightened body grew toward the heavens and with outstretched arms, she grabbed the fragmenting trunk as it fell toward her friends. She grunted under the weight, but succeeded in stopping its plunge. Helen and Cathy collapsed in relief, but Danni wasted no time revealing the truth of the situation.

"Uh, this is pretty heavy!" Her voice boomed, sounding all the more urgent coming from above.

Helen and Cathy worked to untangle themselves with renewed vigor. Kat managed to squirm free of Helen's hair, crawling backwards, away from danger.

"Kat! Help!" Danni pleaded.

Kat chewed her nails. "How?"

"You can cut the tree! Like the desk bar!" Helen shouted.

Branches jabbed into Danni's side and thighs. The coarse trunk scraped against her sweaty palms as she dug her fingers in, determined to hold on.

"Just cut the trunk the rest of the way from the roots so I can toss it!"

Kat removed her jagged fingertips from her mouth and stared at them.

"Kat!" Danni called.

"Hurry!" Helen's voice begged from within the hair.

Strands flew everywhere in an attempt to get free, but they made matters worse by entangling themselves in nearby brush.

Danni held the tree trunk against her waist. She had no strength left to lift it higher or shove it away. Apparently, her brawn was only proportional to her growth and she was not the superwoman she had felt like moments ago. Now, the rough bark slid from her grasp, breaking away as she adjusted her grip. She tugged and tugged to break it off, but the trunk wouldn't budge. It was going nowhere but straight down. Kat stood motionless—or appeared to from Danni's height. Was she refusing to help?

Danni tugged again. Her mind raced for another option. Her friends would be crushed beneath her!

With that pitiful notion, the trunk cracked and splintered from her grip. Danni scrabbled to catch the tumbling pieces, but she was unable to stop the mass from crashing to the ground. She cried out in desperation for her friends.

All was quiet.

Then, beyond Danni's own thudding heartbeat, she heard the sound of brush and twigs crunching underfoot. As the dust and dirt settled from the air, she saw Cathy's faintly glowing form, hopping up and down amongst the litter.

"Cathy! You're okay!"

Danni scooped Cathy up in her tired, scraped-up hands and lifted her little friend to her cheek for a tearful embrace. Cathy fidgeted like a captured frog in her grasp. When Danni located Helen and Kat, Helen was bawling. Her hair was gone.

As Kat's nails retracted to a more manageable size, she pleaded with Helen. "It's okay. It's okay!"

"But—my—ha-air!" Helen sobbed.

Tufts of red jutted from her sheared scalp. Tangled masses of it hung from branches or blew across the ground like tumbleweeds. Danni had been too big and too high up to distinguish Kat's transformation from all of the commotion.

Kat was glowing like everyone else now, and instead of helping Danni, she had cut the other two loose—without permission. Helen hyperventilated in deep, ugly gasps and Kat clamped her hands down on Helen's shoulders to steady her.

"Your hair is fine."

"Mm—But—"

"Helen, make it grow."

Helen quieted. She blinked a few times and her hair began to reappear where it had been chopped the worst. As Helen grasped what was happening, she released a deep sigh of relief.

"I hate you," she said to Kat.

"That's okay."

"Guys?" Danni's voice echoed from above them. "Is everything alright?"

"We're fine," Kat answered. "But I think I've had enough excitement for the night."

Helen sniffed. She craned her neck back to tell Danni, "You look immensely less disturbing in proportion."

Danni chuckled. "Thanks."

"I'd like to go down now," Cathy said.

CHAPTER ELEVEN
"What else are best friends for?"

Danni

As quiet as the girls had been at the beginning of the evening, their near-death experience had enlivened them. They chattered and gestured, interrupting one another, telling and retelling their harrowing tale. The four of them were in various states of reformation, Danni getting shorter by the second, Helen's hair getting longer. Kat was still faintly illuminated, but had no nails to speak of, having chewed them off already. Cathy had managed to find her old self again—she had run off all her pizazz for the time being.

"We should definitely have practice again," Helen declared at a lull in the conversation.

"After what just happened?" Danni said. "You're kidding."

"My reasoning for this first practice still stands, and clearly, we have to get better."

"You almost died," Kat reminded her.

"Next time, Cathy shouldn't go first, that's all."

"Seriously." Danni turned her attention to Cathy, "What was that anyway?"

"It's what always happens." Cathy kicked at the leaf litter. "My brain gets blurry, like I'm thinking too many thoughts at once. It drives me crazy and I can't sit still. I get these sudden bursts of energy."

"Like you're on a sugar high," Danni said.

"Or you have super ADHD," Helen added.

"Oh, great." Cathy threw her hands up in the air. "What am I supposed to do about *that*?"

Helen threw an arm around Cathy's shoulders to comfort her. "You just need to work on your concentration."

"I'd rather work on making it stop."

"I don't think that's an option."

"But I could have gotten us killed!"

"What else are best friends for?"

"Real touching you two," Kat mocked, "but if we ever do this again, we need *a lot* more control."

"Yeah, how did we do it, anyway?" said Danni. "I wasn't even trying when it happened."

When Cathy had no response, Helen reflected, "All I know is, I wanted to help Cathy. And I couldn't do it myself."

"And when I saw that tree about to crush you guys, I had to do *something*. I had to save my friends," Danni added.

When they looked to Kat, she said, "I couldn't do it at first. I mean, you guys were in serious trouble, and nothing happened. So, I thought to myself, over and over, I've got to help Helen and Cathy. Maybe I willed it to happen."

"So, you could help them, but you couldn't help me," Danni said, accusing.

Kat shrugged. "Yeah, I guess."

"I'm sure there's a logical explanation," Cathy said.

"Yeah, she hates me!" said Danni.

"Other than that," Cathy muttered.

Helen jumped ahead to get everyone's attention and keep the peace. "Hey, we're still new at this. There could be any reason."

After that, the girls continued to the house in silence, where parents were already waiting to drive their daughters home. They checked each other to make sure there was no evidence of their ordeal before saying their good-byes. As Cathy and Danni got into their families' vehicles, Kat stalked up the street on her own.

"Is your friend walking home?" Danni's mom asked in a worried voice.

Danni mumbled, "I think so."

"It's dark outside, where does she live?"

Danni answered hesitantly, "Near the school."

"Near the school! *Your* school?" Her mom said, "Go get her, we're giving her a ride."

Danni looked out the rear window to see Cathy's SUV driving away in the opposite direction. It was too late for other options. She got back out of the van to call for Kat. Kat turned around with a scowl.

"We're giving you a ride," Danni called.

"No thanks."

Danni rolled her eyes. "It's not really an option."

Kat was reluctant, but she understood what was going on. There was no way out of it. She trudged back to the Emersons' van and climbed in. "Nice eye roll. Very Priscilla Driscalle."

"My goodness, honey, isn't someone coming to get you?" Danni's mom asked as she started the vehicle.

Kat answered, "Mother's working."

"Well, I suppose we'll take you home then." Danni's mom said matter-of-factly.

Danni had never considered her large family much of a curse until she and Kat were forced to sit in the same back row, due to the number of car seats and sleeping siblings. They rode in silence, but Kat's breath was raspy. Aware that Danni was staring at her, Kat turned her head toward the window and inched closer to the side of the van. Following a particularly loud wheeze, Danni spoke up.

"You've got asthma."

Kat said nothing.

"I do, too."

Danni dug her inhaler out of a back pocket. "If you don't have yours, maybe you can borrow mine?"

"I have it," Kat muttered.

"I had to use mine—" Danni caught herself "—today." Her mom was still watching the road, but Danni spoke more quietly, "I had to use it once I changed back. It didn't bother me until then. I suppose that's a good thing. Can you imagine a giant-sized asthma attack?"

Kat continued brooding at the window.

"It's okay," Danni said. "I know you like to keep your... image...but lots of people have asthma."

Kat wheeled around furiously, catching Danni off guard. "I'm not mad because I have asthma! I'm mad because I have something in common with you."

"I knew it!" Danni exclaimed in a whisper. "You hate me! That's why you couldn't help me with the tree! What did I ever do to you?"

Kat leaned back in her seat, illuminated briefly by the lights of passing cars. "A year ago, Priscilla Driscalle and I were best friends, like Helen and Cathy."

"Yeah, right." Danni was taken aback at Kat's revelation.

"You calling me a liar? We went to school together—me, her, and the rest of them, since kindergarten," Kat began. "But in fifth grade, she changed. She said the things I liked to do were too childish. She started to dress up and look at makeup. She got a phone and didn't want to play games anymore. She wanted to talk about boys—which was weird, because we'd always made fun of that sort of thing—but she was my friend, so..."

Kat showed no trace of emotion to the seat in front of her. But she told her story in a resentful tone.

"When we got together to go shopping for new clothes—I couldn't—I didn't have the money to buy any of the stuff we were looking at. So, I just hung out and didn't try anything on. She kinda made fun of me for it, but I thought maybe she was kidding.

"She started hanging out with me less after that, lying about stuff she had to do. Then, she ignored me. Her and the others. So, I went my way and they went theirs. End of story."

"But what does that have to do with me?"

Kat scoffed. "You're no different than the rest of them. You're just doing what she does, getting in with her group, so you can forget the rest of us. What's the point of being friends with someone who's gonna drop you the minute they don't need you anymore? Leave you alone..."

Danni opened her mouth to defend herself, but her mom interrupted. "Which one is it honey?"

"Third one up," Kat said.

Danni was blocking Kat in, so they both unbuckled their seatbelts. When her mom pulled into Kat's driveway and they got out, Kat added, "You can try your hardest with your fake smiles, your fancy clothes, and your softball team, but once Priscilla's done with you, she'll turn on you like you're a piece of dirt."

Kat left Danni and marched up the driveway without looking back.

Now, it is an established fact that no middle school student actually eats the cafeteria lunches. The period of a child's life during which he enters the apex of physical growth and change is no more than a lie orchestrated by guilty parents who, instead of ensuring a good and wholesome meal themselves, drop a dollar or two into the shaky hands of their underfed child and tell him to buy lunch at the school and to "have a nice day."

As the child's body becomes lanky and awkward due to the lack of proper nutrition, the parents sneak downstairs at night and re-mark the marks on the growth chart, cut slivers of wood from the kitchen furniture, and exclaim in the morning how much their child has grown. When the child leaves for school, similar revisions are made to his bedroom, and his clothes are thrown into a hot water-filled washing machine. All this, to deny the guilt that comes from knowingly subjecting their child to the travesty of the school cafeteria lunch.

It is also an established fact that the quality of the lunch prepared by the high school cafeteria is immensely better than that of the middle school, and the child begins to thrive on his three square meals a day, growing to greater proportions.

They call this process of guilt and lies "puberty."

From *The Collected Conspiracies of Abraham Wong*
Transcribed and edited by Bill

CHAPTER TWELVE

"Little boy"

Linda

First day of school

Linda the lunch lady stared at the industrial-sized dough mixer clanking in front of her. Her horn-rimmed glasses slipped slowly down her rounded nose as the frizzy mass of salt-and-pepper hair battled the regulation net atop her head. Small strands of it tickled her cheek, but her attention was on the growing mass of potato spuds as they toppled around inside the mixer. These were not last year's potatoes. The first shipment of the new school year had arrived in a single box, stamped, "Dehydrated Mashed Generic Potatoes: Made in Taiwan."

The school's principal had been uncharacteristically excited by this shipment. He had thrust the box at the cafeteria workers, telling them to make the mashed potatoes a part of every meal this year.

Linda caught herself glaring at the potatoes now. Her thick glasses magnified the size of her blue eyes tenfold—a formidable glare, indeed. Most people found her gaze unsettling, but the potatoes didn't seem to care.

It was the first day of school, and the other lunch ladies already loved the ease of preparation and the time they saved with these new potatoes, but Linda was not convinced. She was used to peeling and cutting real potatoes—boiling and mashing them herself—but these potatoes were different. She didn't trust them. They lied.

They were lying to her at this very moment! They weren't from Taiwan. Linda knew Taiwanese mashed potatoes. These were not Taiwanese mashed potatoes. Linda was an expert on mashed potatoes. She was an expert on corn, and Salisbury steak, and blueberry crisp. She was an expert on all cafeteria-related things. Her greatest joy in life was creating healthy and nutritious foods for growing children.

She powered down the mixer at the exact time the directions required. The box of dehydrated potato powder was only twelve inches in length on each side, yet it was supposed to be an entire year's supply. Linda had added half of a teaspoon of the de-hydrated flakes to ten gallons of water and now she had more than twenty gallons of the stuff. The physical impossibility of this hurt her brain.

Linda whispered into the bowl of mashed potatoes, "I know you lie. I know!"

"Linda?"

Behind her, the principal had been standing with his arms crossed over his chest, his ever-present scuffed white megaphone dangling from one wrist. What was his name again? After three years in food service at the school, Linda had caught on that the children called him "Principal Pal." It was good enough for Linda, who would have come up with "Principal Shiny-Comb-over" if left to her own devices.

"Are those done?" he asked.

Linda sucked in a lungful of air. "Yes I think they are done but they are not done right because mashed potatoes are not supposed to lie and these mashed potatoes lie because they are not real mashed potatoes—"

Formulating sentences when speaking to actual people was not one of Linda's strong points.

"Right…Well, if they're done, why don't you scoop them onto those trays?"

The principal did not wait for another response, but moved on to the other ladies to check their progress—much more hands-on than usual for this first day of school.

"Almost done?"

"Almost," replied one.

Another tottered over from the pantry, lugging a giant yellow box. "Just adding the cornstarch."

To Linda, her fellow lunch ladies were a group of unnamed white aprons with permed grey hair kept neatly under nets and straggly chin hairs kept discretely under faces. When necessary, she would find distinct features to tell them apart.

After lowering the giant bowl, Linda proceeded to scrape the condescending spuds into a deep plastic tub, which she carried to the hot rack. With an ice cream scooper, she glopped the mashed potatoes onto the Styrofoam trays, already laden with baked lasagna and peach cobbler.

"Double, double, toil and trouble!" the lunch ladies cackled behind her.

Linda spun around, determined. Whatever they were creating, she was sure she had not been included for a reason. As Linda approached, the wart-nosed one added a second box of cornstarch to a large vat. It steamed as the too-much-lipsticked one and the bearded one vigorously stirred with oversized whisks. As the two stirrers rotated, Linda saw a pamphlet on the side of the table where they were working. At the top of the page, she read the word: NEUTRALIZER. Linda gasped and they froze, naughty deer in the headlights of an oncoming lecture.

"Children forgive them for they know not what they do," she crooned.

"It's not what it looks like," explained the bearded one.

They had all been confronted at one time or another by Linda and her abhorrence of unnatural foods.

"The only real ingredient in that is cornstarch!" Linda's mouth was agape.

"It's—It's gravy," blurted the wart-nosed one.

"It must be thrown away!" Linda stammered. "I—I will make gravy."

"No!" The too-much-lipsticked one dashed in front of the tub. "The potatoes—they need *this* gravy."

Linda covered her mouth with the tips of her fingers, wavering where she stood.

The bearded one lifted her hairy chin to see the lunch line. "Students!" she shrieked.

"Quickly, Linda," said the too-much-lipsticked one. "Stall them until we're finished."

"Oh—Oh—Oh no!"

"Linda, you have to!"

Linda scurried to the line. *Fine*, Linda thought, *if you want me to stop them, I'll tell them the truth!*

"Pssst," she said. "Pssssssssstttthth!"

Poking her head above the sneeze guard, Linda gained the attention of two girls in the lunch line, one with long red hair, and another with glasses, who was holding a lunch tray.

"Are we in trouble?" the one with glasses asked.

Linda whispered at her urgently. "Don't get the school lunch."

"She can't help it," the long-haired girl whispered back, unaffected by Linda's warning. "She has to."

"It comes from a box."

The girls had come closer, but Linda had to make sure they knew what they were eating. She grabbed the wrist of the girl who had taken one of the lunches.

"They lie!" she said. "The box—it can't contain them—they grow." How could she explain this to the children? "They need the gravy."

"It's okay. She doesn't like gravy—"

Linda was desperate to make them understand but all she could come up with was: "I watched them make it, toil and trouble. The gravy's almost done!"

"Hey, Linda," the long-haired girl said, "That kid's getting potatoes too!"

"No!" Linda dropped the wrist of the girl with glasses. The two hurried away, but there was no time for them. She got the attention of the new child who had come into the line. "Boy! Little boy!"

The boy stopped in his tracks and glowered at her something awful. Linda was so taken aback that she had no idea what more to say. He picked a tray and trudged away from the lunch line.

Linda held back the tears that were making the meals in front of her abstract and wavy. "Nobody cares," she told the blurry meals. "What can I do?"

She observed the food on the plates: lasagna, mashed potatoes, and peach cobbler. What were these three foods doing together? An Italian main dish should have Caesar salad and tiramisu. Who was planning the menus?

Linda was dreaming up new Italian-inspired recipes when Wart-nose joined her, holding a ladle. She began pouring the opaque, pseudo-liquid substance over the lying potato mounds.

"Did you stop them?" Wart-nose asked.

Linda broke out of her reverie, clueless about what to say. "Lemon-zucchini meatballs," she answered.

Wart-nose arched a penciled-on eyebrow and set her tub of gravy next to the rehydrated dehydrated generic mashed potatoes that lied. She then made her escape from Linda's presence. As the children left the cashier's station, Linda whispered to the substance on the trays beneath her.

"You lie! You are not food but you pretend to be food and I will get you for this. I will fix this school and everything that's wrong with their food."

Tommy

Little boy? Tommy Walker tramped towards the last long table in the cafeteria. There were so many other ways to describe him. "The kid with the buzzed hair and round head," for example.

It was seriously round. His dad often joked about shaving specific patterns in his hair, like a globe or an eight ball. Less than a week ago, his dad had been drawing lines along his scalp and joking.

"*...Here and here. Then, they can just dribble his head down the court! Hah!*"

At school now, Tommy would prefer to be notorious as "that guy who kicks everyone's butt at battle royale," although he would have settled for "the kid with the gamer shirt."

But no. It was never his clothes, or what he was good at, or his oddly spherical head, even. It was always his height. It was always "little boy."

So, he was short. His mom was short. His dad was short. But Tommy was in sixth grade. He'd get bigger, right? His best friend, Zach, had already outgrown him, even though no one in Zach's family was tall either. There was still time. He wouldn't be little Tommy Walker forever, would he?

Tommy was so busy sulking he didn't notice the size thirteen shoe jut into his path. He tumbled and fell flat on his stomach. The students all around him laughed as Tommy pulled his face out of the lasagna that had cushioned his fall. His eyes were stinging from the red sauce and they blinked shut to tear away the pain.

Not tears! Not here!

Tommy forced his lids open, just a slit, to peek up at the boy who had tripped him.

The giant mountain of a boy balled his fists against his cheeks, mockingly. "Are you sure you're s'posed to be in middle school, little guy?"

More laughter.

Tommy didn't answer. He crawled to his feet and wiped himself off as best he could. Then, he lumbered to the nearest table. Would he be little Tommy Walker forever? The answer, apparently, was yes.

He chose a seat at the end and examined what had survived of his lunch. Most of the lasagna was on his forehead, and his peach cobbler was a chunky puddle on the floor. His milk carton had burst open under a table, and his mashed potatoes had—

Stayed where they were?

Gross.

The dome-shaped scoop of mashed potatoes was smooshed to the side a little, but it had clung to the tray somehow. Thankful that he wouldn't starve, Tommy wiped his spork on his shirt and dug in.

Tommy didn't look up as Zach sat down across from him. It wasn't enough that his best friend was taller than him, but girls thought he was cute, too. One of the girls in their English class had told him he should do K-pop. Zach had immediately proved her wrong with the world's worst rendition of "I Want It that Way."

"What happened to your lunch?" Zach asked.

"Big kid," Tommy responded through mouthfuls of potato spuds.

It was hard to speak with the strange potato substance sticking to the roof of his mouth and doing who-knew-what to his tongue. His mouth felt fuzzy, almost tingly. These clearly weren't made from scratch mashed potatoes. They weren't even tolerable mashed potatoes. Without milk, he smacked his gums crudely.

Zach dug into his lunch bag. "Here, you can have my granola bar and share my drink-ade."

Little Tommy Walker was thankful for Zachary Park and his granola bar. As he munched the sugary snack, Tommy realized he may never be big, but he hoped he would find a way to stand up to those big kids. Otherwise, it was going to be a long year.

CHAPTER THIRTEEN
"The power of the fruit"

Tommy
Second week of school

Tommy Walker could barely move his legs. He had been wobbly over the weekend, but it had usually passed after breakfast. He was tired. Very tired. He thought soda might help wake him up, but he had no money for the vending machines. To top this off, Tommy was hungry, like he hadn't eaten breakfast at all. At least the hungry part he could do something about.

He took one of the ready-made lunch trays from the shelf, surprised he was even able to lift its weight. It was an open-faced something sandwich, buried in mashed potatoes and slathered with gravy. To one side, sat a pile of corn and above it, a chunk of what appeared to be cornbread. After the first day, he vowed he wouldn't touch those weird potatoes ever again—gravy or no gravy. So, it looked like lunch was going to be very corny.

As he lowered the food, he was met by a pair of giant-sized eyeballs. He stiffened and clenched the edges of the lunch tray. *Not her again.*

The eccentric lunch lady spoke. "You look terrible little boy."

"Tommy. My name's Tommy."

"Linda. My name is Linda."

"Thanks," Tommy muttered.

He turned to go, but she spoke again. "What's wrong little boy?"

Tommy winced, but answered anyway. He was too exhausted to resist. "I'm so tired. Is there something to help me wake up?"

"You want sugar?" said the eyes and the mound of frizzy hair.

"Yeah, maybe that'd work."

The lunch lady extended her neck like a turtle coming out of its shell. "Did you know fruit is sweet and full of fiber and *natural* sugars?" she asked.

"Uh, maybe?"

"That will help you I think."

Tommy reviewed the food in front of him with a disappointed grunt. Linda assessed his tray.

"You lie!" she hissed.

"What?"

"Nothing," she spat, in an angry tone.

"Is corn a fruit?"

"Technically sometimes."

The conversation died.

Linda pursed her lips and said, "You want fruit I'll get you fruit wait a minute."

Linda disappeared, leaving Tommy hesitant to wait for her. He had barely understood her last nervous statements. She returned carrying an apple and a banana, which she shoved under the sneeze guard.

"Quickly take these and go!"

"Thanks!"

Tommy snatched the pieces of fruit and stuffed them in his pockets. He scooped up his tray and left the lunch line with as much speed as his tired legs could carry him.

Tommy
Third week of school

If an apple a day could keep the doctor away, Tommy Walker would never see a stethoscope again. By the third week of the school year, the extra fruit on his daily lunch tray had gone from a couple of pieces to a pile. When Zach finally questioned his friend's new eating habits, Tommy explained:

"I can feel the power of the fruit surging within me. Where once I was tired and weak, now I am awake and strong. Each day, I drag myself into school, slow, lacking the motivation to move, to reason. My body craves something—something to give it the fuel to function. Thanks to the lunch lady, Linda, I now know that something is the secret, life-giving sugar of the fruit-plant.

"Now, I rise in the morning yearning for the vitality of the sun, the food of the earth. I used to be little, helpless. But, as I partake of this wondrous bounty, I am stronger, better—not like a boy, but like a man! A fruit man!"

Tommy gazed into a vague distance, letting the thoughts swirl around in his head.

Zach snapped his fingers and when Tommy blinked back into focus, Zach asked him again if he was alright.

"Ah, I don't know…"

Forced to examine the words that were actually coming out of his mouth, Tommy sifted through his own inner monologue. Everything revolved around this craving for energy and the fruit that fulfilled it.

He continued. "My brain gets fuzzy. Sometimes, I can manage okay. Other times, I…feel…tough as the core of the apple!" Tommy was gone again. "As hard as the rind of the ripe watermelon!"

"Tommy, you're not even eating watermelon."

"Zesty as the juice of the orange…"

Linda

Papers littered the floor of the small, cluttered room. Ancient filing cabinets the school had discarded long ago were lined up along the short wall. Some of their drawers hung open, revealing recipe after recipe: cream of papaya soup; chicken a la vizier, with mint sauce; sugar-free, chocolate-free, gluten-free, black bean raisin brownies.

The other wall was filled with books, stacked haphazardly on top of one another. Titles such as *The Lost Art of Flavor Combination* and *The King's Guide to French Cuisine* were barely legible in the dim light. Scattered notes and kitchen appliance guides covered what space was left on the walls, and dusty curtains covered the only window to the tiny room, keeping the outside world out and the inside world in.

Linda sat at an old secretary's desk in a tired chair with flattened cushions. A rickety typewriter perched on the desktop, next to a heap of notebooks and a soup can full of pencils. Her work uniform bumped around in the dryer down the hall. She may have been a nutrition expert, but she occasionally forgot to eat, herself. Oftentimes, Linda found her work was consuming her instead. This weekend would be no different.

As she rocked back and forth in the noisy chair, Linda muttered, incensed and frustrated. She saw children drinking nothing but fizzy pop and juice-flavored high fructose corn syrup. They ate sugary fake-cakes and greasy, salty snacks.

The school lunch, what should have been a shining beacon of nutrition in the pitch-black world of unhealthy substitutes, was wholly lacking.

The little boy to whom she had been sneaking fruit was the last straw. She had been trying to help him, but could no longer give him what he needed. The other lunch ladies had caught on to the missing food and they were suspicious, since they never used the fruit themselves. When the other lunch ladies got suspicious, they always blamed Linda for some reason.

A shiny red apple was nestled in the pocket of Linda's worn cardigan. She spoke to it as she considered her options.

Linda had to do something now, before it was too late. "The students must be fed the right foods. No more foods that lie!" The dull bulb in her decades-old lamp flickered. "Yes. They must be taught a lesson but how? What will show them their mistakes? What will make them listen to me?"

Linda pulled her typewriter forward. Its feet scraped the worn desktop.

"I don't know why I talk to you," she told the apple. "You never answer me."

How could she make them listen?

"I must act. I must do something big."

She would do something big. Linda lifted a decided, but shaky finger, and tapped the first key. The typewriter slammed the letter forth into the paper. The inky splotch startled Linda, but she swallowed hard and pressed a second letter and a third...

Tommy
Fourth week of school

In the following days, Tommy went through many highs and lows. Before lunch, he was sickly, but by the end of the period and throughout the rest of the day, He would be fine, if not a little quirkier. That is, until the day Tommy ate his last apple.

As he and Zach shuffled through the masses on their way to their next class, Tommy felt his grip weaken on his textbooks. Somewhere in his mind he thought to catch them, but every part of his body—from the neurons that deliver such messages, to the knuckles that would have carried out the order—was utterly exhausted.

Zach reacted to the dropped books faster than Tommy, but not before the students behind them kicked Tommy's math book down the hallway. Zach shouted for them to stop, and the bigger kids went on their way, high-fiving each other. Tommy's movements were strained and sluggish. Zach helped him to the side of the hallway and asked what was wrong.

"The fruit is not enough anymore. I tried to get more from Linda, but she sent me away. She said I was taking too much now and she couldn't keep sneaking me more food. What am I gonna do, Zach? I can barely walk."

"Did you tell your parents?"

Tommy scoffed. "I told them I wanted to eat fruit all the time and Dad said he wouldn't be caught dead raising a vegan."

"What about the nurse?"

"She gave me this." Tommy lifted up his shirt and there was a Band-Aid on his stomach.

Tommy's face was ashen. He slid down the wall to sit on the floor as Zach dug into his backpack

"I was saving this for later, but maybe it'll help."

He handed Tommy a leftover snack cake from his lunch. As the rest of the student body passed by obliviously, Tommy took a bite of the sweet snack. He felt his body assault the cake as it reached his stomach. Acids frothed it apart and energy surged out. Warmth returned to his skin. He took another ravenous bite and his shoulders lifted. Tommy finished off the rest of the snack, stuffing it between his snapping teeth, letting its sweet cake and sugary filling revive him. He gathered his books and jumped to his feet.

. . . .

The next day at lunch, Zach shared his snack again and Tommy revealed to him that he had made a plan: "I have devised a way to fuel this endless hunger of mine. It is clear to me now that I must consume a certain quantity of sugar in order to function, and I happen to know where there is an everlasting supply!"

"Great..." Zach said. "What's with all the, uh, words?"

"I have no idea," Tommy confessed. His racing thoughts and singular focus were running away with his mouth. "But this sugar supply—I need your help to obtain it."

Zack ran his fingers through his hair and scratched his scalp. As Tommy waited for an answer, he was dimly aware of how much craziness he was loading into their friendship.

"…Okay."

"Yes!" That dim awareness vanished as Tommy rose from his seat and cried, "I shall be the mighty Fruit Man! And you shall be my Fruity Henchman! Ha ha ha!"

"But you're not eating fruit anymore, Tommy."

CHAPTER FOURTEEN
"School hierarchy"

Kat
Week five, now

Helen had been talking for a while now, but Kat was too busy with her own observations to pay attention. Kat's mind wandered as she watched the noisy cafeteria. The four of them sat in the same place, but the groups around them were constantly changing.

"...So, I got my parents to agree to let me have everyone over again today, so long as I get my homework done..."

The people further down the table were not the same ones who had been there at the beginning of the year. Nor were the people at the table across the aisle. Friendships had been made and broken already. It was confusing.

"...I don't think anyone really explores the forest and most of the hair has become one with nature. So, we can meet up and take the bus to my house again. Danni will show up sometime after softball practice..."

Helen sure did talk a lot. *Squawk squawk, little parrot.*

"I guess you guys will need to leave before dinner—"

"Who are we?" Kat interrupted.

"'Scuse me?"

At least when you are stereotypical, you know where you belong, Kat thought. "Who are we?" she asked again.

"I'm Helen," came the reply. "You're Kat..."

"No." Kat crossed her arms.

"I'm not sure I get the question."

"So, there's them." Kat gestured discretely with her thumbs. "And them."

"School hierarchy," Cathy translated.

"Oh!" Helen's expression brightened.

Cathy seemed to know what was coming. "Oh boy, here we go..."

"See, I've given this some thought," Helen said, "and the way I see it, there are a couple basic groups within the middle school hierarchy."

Danni had stopped munching on her sandwich crust and Kat propped her chin on her fists, listening.

"First, there are the populars—the Eloi."

"No one else has read that book," Cathy whispered.

Helen flippantly waved her comment away. "Those are the people who know people, who know people, you know? Like, Priscilla Driscalle has her gaggle, and Misha Thompson has her gaggle. Even Andrea Sodders has her gaggle in class with Cathy and me. But they're interconnected. They network; they jump back and forth.

"Sport players—they're Eloi, too. Kids with money—"

"Wait! I play a sport," Danni remarked.

"Yeah, but you're in band. They cancel each other out."

Danni averted her eyes and stuck out her lower lip.

"What's wrong with band?" Cathy whimpered.

Helen continued. "And then there's the lowest group, the exiles, if you will. They're the nerds, the ones who like stuff that has no interest to the majority of the population."

"Cah-Cahomic books," Danni coughed.

"Anyhoo…" Helen cast a sideways glance at Danni. More than likely, Helen had comics in her backpack even as she spoke. "They're boring to everyone but their own kind. Sometimes, you'll find the castaways in this group, too. The ones who did one stupid thing in their brief time here to make them outcasts."

Danni jumped in to add, "Remember Sean Hagleman, Tina Hagleman's brother? It's one thing to get sick and throw up—I mean, *we* have, but his came out the *other* end. In the middle of passing period."

Helen nodded. "And that's branded him disgusting. Now people say he has b.o. and peeling scabs. And there was the girl who brought a teddy bear to school on her first day. That didn't go well."

"I think she cried," Danni added.

"Now she sits by herself every day like she was dropped on a deserted island."

"Helen, you're terrible," Cathy said.

"I'm just telling unfortunate truths. As the year goes on, I bet we'll see more castaway-exiles."

"What about them?" Kat thumbed over her shoulder.

The others followed her finger to a round table with three students in mixed grades. They wore mostly black clothes, in varying styles. Each had dark or black hair, and skin made pale in contrast to their severe style choices.

"Morlocks."

"Helen!"

"Exiles," She explained, "People stay away from them. S'got nothing to do with their personalities, 'cause nobody tries to get to know them, what with the scariness and all."

"Scariness?" Kat asked in a monotone.

Helen was oblivious to her mood.

"I mean, isn't that what they're going for? I don't really get it myself—"

"So, who are we?" Kat asked again.

Helen considered her question. "We're the space takers. We're the ones in between, without ties to any particular group, or maybe more than one group." She gestured. "We sit here between the gaggles and the geeks, the Eloi and the exiles, taking up space at the lunch table."

"Great," Kat said. This had been entirely useless.

"Speaking of which," Cathy added. "Where were you at lunch yesterday?"

Kat stood up to throw away her trash, looking down on the geek, the nerd, and the fashionista she was spending her time with.

"With the Morlocks," she said.

Linda

Linda pushed her glasses back up onto the bridge of her nose and stretched to reach the casserole pans stacked on the top shelf of the walk-in refrigerator. The label stared her in the face, mocking her:

Ready-Made Tuna Casserole
Ingredients: Enhanced Fish Meat Byproduct, High-Fructose Corn Syrup, Semolina, Carrageenan, Sodium Nitrate, Maltodextrin, Artificial Cheese Flavoring, Preservatives (proprietary blend)

Like today's tuna casserole, the majority of the food in the walk-in had a shelf life of several years, made to be prepared quickly and cheaply. Linda was disgusted by most of it. From the tips of her toes, on the slippery tile floor, she gripped the sides of the bottom pan with her fingertips. She carefully slid the stack to the edge of the shelf, but the top pans slipped forward, tipping and falling toward the floor.

"Oh!"

Linda ducked as one pan crashed and spilled open at her feet. The other skidded along the floor and under the back shelves. Linda's glasses fell around her neck, dangling from their chain. Flustered, she shimmied around the mess she had made and tiptoed to the back of the refrigerator. She crouched on the floor and felt for the other pan, hoping it had not also been ruined. The principal had been more concerned with food cost this year.

The large, chilly room was shaped like an L, with the shorter side blocked off by thick strips of hanging plastic. Its lights flickered eerily. They had been doing so for weeks and Linda had been told this was due to faulty wiring that would be repaired eventually. The entire side around the corner was dark, which made locating the fallen casserole pan difficult.

As Linda searched for the second tray, a sharp and putrid stench hit her nose. She cleared her throat and put a hand on the tile to steady herself. The cold, gungy floor embraced her palm, causing goosebumps to ripple up her arm. A slimy sauce had pooled out from the dark side of the L.

Linda reached for her glasses with her clean hand then pulled the hanging plastic aside. The lights flickered once again, and the area around the corner lit up. The other lunch ladies came running when they heard her scream.

CHAPTER FIFTEEN
"You got a problem?"

Tommy

Tommy's face almost hit the table when someone came up behind him and smacked him in the back of the head. He knew instinctively who the culprit was.

"Well, well, if it isn't the shortest kid is school."

"Hey!" Zach said.

Zach pushed away from the table, but Tommy stopped him with a gesture.

"It's okay. I've got this."

His friend remained seated as Tommy faced the attacker. It was the same kid who had been dogging him all semester, Greg Schultz.

Tommy thrust out his chin. "You got a problem?"

"What?" Greg said, cupping a hand to his ear. "Did somebody say something? I thought I heard a tiny voice."

Tommy sprung to his feet. "At least I don't pick on people who are smaller than me!"

"Kid, there is no one smaller than you."

The students around them snickered and Tommy shrunk from his failed attempt at bravado. Greg pushed him back into his seat. A steady diet of pilfered junk food had made Tommy feel stronger than ever, but even now, it seemed he was still helpless.

Overcome by the desire to hurt someone—to prove he was tough enough to stand up to Greg's insults—Tommy grabbed a food item from nearby and pulled his arm back, aiming at the bully.

Greg whooped hysterically and sauntered away. "What're you gonna do? Beat me up with a muffin?"

At this point, most children would have given up. But not Tommy Walker. Greg the bully should not have been so quick to turn his back on Tommy and his muffin, for Tommy threw the muffin anyway—no longer a soft, tasty pastry. Gripped within the palm of his hand, the muffin's construction had changed. The small object had solidified and crystallized as Tommy poured his anger and frustration into it.

By the time the once-muffin had sailed through the air and connected with the back of Gregory Schultz's cranium, it had the weight and consistency of a brick.

The muffin bounced off his head and smashed to pieces upon hitting the floor. Greg hit his knees and fell forward. The area silenced. Greg's friends rushed to check on him.

As they rolled him over, Greg slurred, "When's supper, mother?"

Every head swiveled in Tommy's direction.

Tommy did not respond. He had a crazed expression and a grin cracked across his lips. When one of the lunch attendants rushed over and asked who was responsible, every finger was pointed at Tommy.

"Get him to the nurse," the attendant said to Greg's friend. "And, you, come with me."

"Can I have my binkie?" Greg asked. "If I'm good?"

Tommy didn't say a word as he was led away toward the principal's office, but when he looked back at Zachary, his grin had grown fiendish and his countenance, frightening.

Linda

With her coworkers gathered around, Linda panted sporadically into the paper bag they had given her. "The moldy fruit... The rotting produce!"

Her vision had collapsed into a tunnel where she could see nothing but the putrid massacre—the dead and dying fruits and vegetables, decomposing and sloughing off their shelves from ignorant disuse. The ladies argued with each other.

"I told you messing with the lights wouldn't be enough."

"Who sent her in there, anyway?

"You knew?" Linda asked.

"Of course we knew," snapped the too-much-lipsticked one.

"Why? Why the waste?"

"Who needs blueberries, when we have prepackaged and naturally flavored blueberry crisp?" Too-much-lipstick gestured to the pantry. "Who needs corn on the cob, when we have cans and cans of creamed corn substitute?"

Linda gagged.

"It'll be okay, Linda." The bearded one put a scraggly hand on her shoulder.

"Yes," the wart-nosed one agreed. "Maybe you can order some bananas next week."

Linda squeezed her shaking knuckles tightly together. "They will only be wasted again."

"That's right," said the too-much-lipsticked one. "We've already cancelled the auto-order. There will be no more fruit or vegetables coming into this kitchen outside of a can!"

Linda seized her coworker by the arms. Linda's wild hair was a frizzy frame around her furious bugged eyes.

Words spewed from her mouth like a magician's scarf trick. "How dare you I will order the fruits and vegetables I will pay for them myself the children must have good food!"

The other two backed away on fearful tiptoes and the too-much-lipsticked one shook in her grasp.

"You will be sorry for this," Linda whispered. Her lower lip quivered as she released her coworker. "Excuse me I must go— And plan."

Without another word to her coworkers, Linda left for the day, returning home to her cluttered little room.

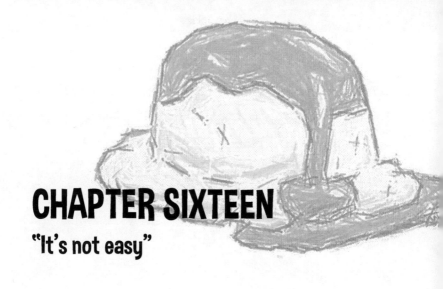

CHAPTER SIXTEEN
"It's not easy"

Helen

The next morning, Helen scribbled answers onto a wrinkled piece of notebook paper, the first to arrive, as usual. She lived on the same street as New Potentia's mayor, and rode the bus with his son. The bus was never late, and in fact, difficult for her dragging, sleepy self to catch most mornings. In the empty math class, Helen hastily completed the homework that was due in the next few minutes.

"X equals eight," Helen wrote the number, without showing her work, and skipped to the next problem. "Y minus three equals ten? So, Y equals…seven—no, thirteen."

Cathy arrived. "Did you see? Two more vending machines were broken into last night."

"Hmm-mm." Helen's nose was in her math book. "The square root of x is nine? Oh, heck on it!" She scratched the number ninety-nine.

Cathy leaned over her. "It's eighty-one."

"Thanks." Helen erased her hasty guess. "Hey, did you get thirteen for the one before that?"

"I got seven."

"Seven?"

"Well," Cathy pulled out her homework. "I wasn't exactly in the best condition for doing math last night."

"Oh. Maybe we can compare."

"Good idea."

They matched each other's papers and chose which answers were best. Helen could see that her friend's performance had, indeed, slipped.

"What are these drawings on your paper?" she asked, referring to the circles and lines in the margins. Helen held up the sheet, squinting at one of the scribbled drawings. "Looks like octopuses."

"Can you just help me erase them?"

"So, I've been thinking," Helen said as she obliged. "Next practice should be this weekend."

Cathy sighed. "I guess."

"I know you don't enjoy it, but it's helping. You're getting better at your school work, right?"

"Yeah," Cathy answered, "But it's not easy."

"It'll get better with practice, like playing the flute."

"But I have to concentrate twice as hard to get the work done. My brain is tired."

Helen consoled her friend, "If anyone can push through it, it's you." More students entered the classroom and she ducked back into her book. "Shoot, we better get this done."

. . . .

At lunch, Helen told Danni of her plans. "But we can't use my house again, because they've got park service crews cleaning up the new mess we made yesterday."

"My parents are a little sick of the mess I've already been making," Cathy said.

"Danni?"

Danni tittered to herself. "Oh, you're serious? There's no such thing as privacy at my house."

"Oh," Helen said, disappointed. "Well, where's Kat?"

"How would I know?" Danni asked.

"Maybe I'll see her in art." Helen wondered if Kat was sick or had skipped. She skimmed the faces in the cafeteria. "Aha! I'll be back."

She made her way to a round table at the back of the room, where Kat was eating her vended lunch with the three students Helen had earlier described as "Morlocks." They frowned as she approached and Kat fit right in, despite her blonde hair.

"Do you know this person, Kat?" asked the tall one to Kat's left.

"Yeah," Kat answered. "Helen, this is Jason, his brother Ben, and Miranda."

Jason was the tallest of the three, an eighth grader. He and his brother had matching straight black hair, though Ben's was longer, covering his eyes. Jason wore a thick black hoodie atop baggy cargo pants. His little brother wore a T-shirt bearing the name of a band Helen had never heard of. Miranda was a tiny face under a thick layer of curly hair. She wore numerous piercings around her ears and thick black mascara and lipstick. She glowered at Helen as Kat explained.

"I didn't feel like sitting there today."

"That's okay," Helen said, "I just have a question."

"Okay."

"We're all gonna—" Helen noted her Morlock audience, "—gonna *get together* this weekend, but we need somewhere to do it."

Kat raised an eyebrow. "You're seriously asking me?"

"Why not?"

The question felt simple enough to Helen, but Kat mulled it over for a peculiarly long time before she answered.

"Mother leaves for work at three on Saturday."

"So, we'll meet in the morning?"

"So, I'll see you at three-thirty."

Jason didn't wait for Helen to leave before asking Kat, "You're, like, friends with her?"

Kat narrowed her eyes. "Yeah?"

Ben lifted his chin to Helen and his hair fell away from his eyes. "YSLF fan?"

Helen grabbed the bottom of her favorite shirt to stretch out the image for all to see. "Yeah! I got this at a convention!"

"How am I still surrounded by geeks?" Kat said under her breath.

"Hey, whatever, man. To each her own." Jason reached an open and expectant palm to Miranda. "Lemme see that black nail polish."

Miranda opened her backpack and pulled out a small bottle, which she handed to Jason. "Kat, you should try this," she said. "It's, like, eight dollars a bottle, but it dries in no time—I mean, it's cool. Makes your nails look like death."

Kat wrinkled her brow at Miranda. "I don't paint my nails."

Jason gave her the bottle anyway. "Try it."

Once it was clear that Kat and the Morlocks were done with her, Helen wandered back to her usual table. "I'll, uh…I'll tell the others."

Cathy

In class after lunch, Cathy blew awkwardly at the lip plate of her flute. The noises she made could hardly be called music, but the point was not to produce music. The band was playing their scales, which she was supposed to know by now. The notes Cathy was producing could hardly be called scales either.

Cathy hoped Mr. Hoffman couldn't hear her mistakes over the other students' instruments. Danni and her trumpet seemed to have no trouble maintaining with the rest of the class. Cathy was jealous of her ability to perform basic tasks with all that was happening to them. She shook her head and focused on the notes in front of her.

Concentration came to Cathy with more and more difficulty these days. She found herself zoning out or following random tangents at a whim. She would fidget uncontrollably, sometimes jolting up and bounding around the room. Cathy never understood what made her do these chaotic things, except that they made sense to her at the time.

To make matters worse, her grades were slipping. The time spent mind-wandering in class and jittering around her room was time that should have been spent paying attention and doing homework. Cathy was losing sleep at night, plagued by strange dreams or staying awake to do work that should have been easy. Recently, she had managed to score an eighty-nine, despite writing the word "chocolate" as one of her answers to a multiple-choice math test.

Helen had scored a ninety-five. Their scores used to be the other way around, with Cathy doing a little better than Helen. While Cathy wasn't so selfish that she couldn't be happy for Helen and Danni in their accomplishments, she was sickened that she was losing ground at the one thing she had over her friends and siblings—academics.

Cathy hated what was happening to her. And the more she thought about it, the more she hated her own terrible luck for once again getting the hand-me-downs of the group. Helen, Kat, and Danni had abilities that affected them physically, but dispelled with concentration. Whatever was happening to Cathy never went away. It was ruining her life.

As she stared at the music in her booklet, Cathy swore that she was seeing enigmatic symbols in place of all the notes. She squeezed her eyes shut and blinked them back open to make the shapes go away.

Cathy felt herself sob once and broke out of her reverie as the music stopped playing. Mr. Hoffman scanned the room and pointed a suspicious wand at her.

"Cathy," he ordered. "Play the scales."

Cathy gulped. "Alone?"

"Yes, if you can."

Cathy brought the shaking flute to her lips. Danni gave her an encouraging thumbs-up from across the room. She inhaled slowly, willed herself to focus, and played her scales.

CHAPTER SEVENTEEN
Click

Danni

The Saturday sun hung at high noon, observing the softball game below and its new outfielder, Danni Emerson, whose team was playing its first game against a rival school. Though she hadn't seen much action here in right field, she would be ready for it when it came. After her fabulous catch during dodge ball, her teammates were still expecting to see amazing things from Danni, and Danni was not about to let them down.

The bases were loaded when a stocky girl got up from the visitors' box and strode toward home plate. Danni prayed she would get her chance. She was moved to imagine her family's pride when she saved the day, the pat on her back from Coach Calhoun, the cheers from her teammates—The invitations to parties, trips to the mall, and the seat—finally—at Priscilla's table! The girl stepped up to the plate and hoisted her bat up onto her shoulder—her left shoulder. Danni could not contain her glee. A left-hander! Now was her chance.

Priscilla glanced in Danni's direction, warning her. She then wound up and tossed the ball directly into the catcher's waiting glove. Strike. There were cheers from the home team's fans, but Danni grumbled under her breath. There was another pitch, and another call from the umpire. Strike two. If Priscilla threw another strike, Danni's hopes would be dashed like so many leaky ships upon a stormy cliff-side sea shore. She watched intensely as Priscilla wound up for the final pitch.

Priscilla's ball whizzed toward the catcher, but it was miraculously intercepted by the rival's swing. There was the *whump* of the bat, and the ball sailed like a dream in her direction. Danni followed the ball's path, striding backwards to intercept it in its fall to the ground. Danni's arms rose instinctively. Her glove opened up to accept this gift of immortal popularity.

Time stood still. The softball rotated gently in the dusty air. The notes of songbirds hung heavily in her ears. The beams of the overhead sun haloed the ball as it drifted toward Danni's glove. Yes, the ball was hers.

Time began its slow creep back to reality. The hum of the crowd picked up as the ball dropped directly to Danni's outstretched hands and...

Click.

. . . .

Cathy, Kat, and Helen were gathered on the curb when the Emersons' van pulled into Kat's driveway. The three had been waiting for their friend, throwing rocks into a nearby drainage grate. They met Danni as she crawled out of the van to the cacophony of crying siblings. She carried a small sports bag and still wore her softball uniform which, along with her face, was covered in dirt and dust. Blades of grass clung to Danni's hair and she walked with an uncharacteristic slouch and a frown. Her mom said some words of encouragement before she pulled away.

Kat was the first to greet her: "You're late."

"What happened?" asked Cathy.

Danni related her softball game experience to her friends. "Priscilla said I was so tall and lanky I looked like an ostrich with my head in the dirt."

Kat chortled.

"Everyone laughed." Danni added.

"I'm real sorry," Helen said.

"Yeah," agreed Cathy.

"That was the first inning. I didn't play any more, but I had to stay for the whole thing. My mom took me out for ice cream. But needless to say, I'm off the team"

"So, you'll be on time from now on?" Kat asked.

"Kat!" Helen snapped.

"I was just asking."

Kat led them up the sidewalk and pushed on the front door. When it didn't budge, she jiggled the handle, perturbed.

"You locked us out?" Cathy asked.

"No." She twisted the door handle again, unsuccessful. "Gimme a sec." Kat brushed past them, whispering to Danni, "I told you..." as she headed around the garage to get to the back of the house.

"Maybe we could practice ignoring your duck-o-meter today," Helen said.

Danni groaned. "Would you quit calling it that?"

"What would we do? Spend the day throwing things at Danni?" asked Cathy. "Kat would like that."

"Yeah, I'm gonna have to admit it," Helen said, "she might hate you."

"What's taking so long?" Danni muttered.

The door in front of them clicked. Kat opened it and stepped aside so they could enter.

"Cool." Helen was the first to cross the threshold. "How'd you get in?"

Kat removed her fingernail from between her teeth to answer. "Bedroom window."

Cathy was next, followed by Danni, who exchanged scowls with Kat. Danni had no idea what to expect when she saw Kat's bedroom, but as she walked down the messy hallway to the room at the back of the house, a flutter of excitement developed in her stomach. Danni had been secretly looking forward to this, as if something in Kat's room would somehow explain her personality. Kat hesitated to open the door, like she could feel everyone's eager stares.

The room's lack of cohesion dumbfounded Danni. Whatever she had been expecting, this was not it. The dresser was messy, and there was a pile of junk at the floor of the closet, as if someone had scraped the room clean in a hurry.

A stack of CDs ranging from heavy metal to pop teetered unsteadily next to an old stereo, against a wall covered in posters. A stuffed animal had been hastily hidden beneath the bedclothes—an old floral comforter that couldn't have been Kat's choice, over mismatched sheets. The window had been closed and the curtains pulled shut.

"Oh, cool!" Cathy said, observing Kat's poster-covered walls. "You like Las Noctámbulas! Bet you're bummed they broke up, huh?"

Kat shrugged. "Which one were they?"

"Why do you have a poster for it if you don't follow the band?" Danni asked.

Kat evaluated her wall. She tore down the poster, rolled it up, and handed it to Cathy with indifference.

"Uh, thanks?" Cathy said, confused.

"So, are we gonna get started or what?" said Kat.

CHAPTER EIGHTEEN
"Not perfect, but better"

Helen

In time, a normal routine formed. Helen and her friends would get together on a regular basis to hone their skills in an attempt to control the phenomena happening to them. They practiced at one another's homes as time would dictate and family would allow. One evening, they managed to meet in Cathy's basement, where they hoped they would not be disturbed. Each had made progress in taming her abilities, and the girls were becoming more confident they could keep their secret hidden, even in such close quarters.

"Twenty-one, twenty-two, twenty-three..." Helen counted.

"Twwenty ooonnneee, twwenty twooo, twwenty threee..." Cathy repeated, in a Zen-like state.

"Twenty-four, twenty-five, twenty-six…"

"Twwenty fooouuuurrrr, twwenty fiiiivvve, piiiieee…"

"Twenty-seven—"

"Okay that is so it!" Danni shouted, startling Helen and Cathy from their exercise and meditation. "Let's do something else, shall we?"

"What's wrong with what we're doing?"

"It's getting on my nerves!" Danni said.

"Everybody's nerves," added Kat.

Helen had been lifting a small table from the floor to the ceiling with her hair in an attempt to test how much weight it could handle. She had started with a set of small barbells, then upgraded to a couple of broken kitchen appliances, followed by the table.

"I was gonna try the old recliner next," she said.

"Don't you daaaaarrrrrre," came Cathy's response.

She was cross-legged on the floor, transformed. The goal was simply to remain calm and repeat after Helen. Occasionally, Danni or Kat would ask her a question that required an uncomplicated, straightforward answer to see if she could also operate with sanity while in this state.

"What do you suggest we do instead?" Helen asked Danni.

"First, Cathy could stop the annoying chanting."

"Are you kidding? This is the best we've seen her in weeks."

"And that's saying something," said Kat.

"I aaaaaammm still in the rooooooooommmmm."

Helen turned to Cathy, "What is another name for 'dog?'"

"Caninnneeee."

"And the rain in Spain?"

"Falls maaaiiinnly on the plaaaaaaiiiiiiinnnnnn."

"I invented gravity when an apple fell on my head. Who am I?"

"Fig Newtonnnnnnn."

"See?" Helen gestured. "Not perfect, but better."

"I guess, but still…" Danni said. "Hey, Cathy, is that your sister's painting?"

"Shh. Don't harsh her vibe," Helen whispered. "But yeah, that's the one she ruined."

Helen set the table back on the floor as the others inspected the painting. What had once been a delicate landscape was now overdrawn by harsh permanent marker, multiple colors mixed together. A large circle took up most of the canvas. Another circle was against the top inside it, with a horizontal line underneath. Two more lines came out at angles from the middle.

"I think it looks like a pie." Helen was matter-of-fact. "With a bite taken out."

"Maybe it's a sun," Danni mused, "with its light shining down. See?" She pointed.

"What about you, Kat?" Helen asked.

Kat tilted her head. "Crescent moon."

Helen micromanaged her hair, using meticulous movements to fold the table legs back together so she could put it away. "Anyhoo, let's try controlling Cathy's outbursts instead of suppressing them next time."

Cathy broke from her trance. "Oh, goodie."

Ignoring her growing headache, Helen said, "We should move on to something else before we break for the night. Why don't Cathy and I help you two test your powers?"

"So, we're calling them powers now?" Kat asked, crossing her arms.

"I'm not comfortable with that," Danni said.

Helen didn't miss a beat. "It's just a word. Something all-encompassing to say to refer to the massive jumble of things that are happening to us."

Danni rabbit-eared quotes in the air as she spoke. "The word 'powers' makes it sound like something cool. Our 'powers' are lame."

Helen's jaw dropped at the offense. "You don't think growing twenty feet tall is cool?"

"I look ridiculous. And so do you, with your hair all over the place."

"What? Kat, do I look ridiculous?"

Kat raised an eyebrow at Helen.

"Well, I think *your* powers are cool," Helen pouted.

"What about me?" Cathy asked.

Helen stared. "Okay, maybe Danni has a point."

Every night they practiced was another night Helen spent keeping her excitement in check. If she wanted the others to ever accept what they could become, she had to walk a fine line between training them and joining in their skepticism. A few more "slipups" and everyone would be using the word "powers" before they knew it.

Helen gave her friends no more time to reflect on what she had said. She zipped a tendril of her hair across the room and lifted Danni's purse from the floor. She hoisted the small, shiny bag up to the ceiling and dangled it over Danni's head.

"Come get it," Helen taunted.

Danni didn't budge for Helen's childish antics.

"C'mon, get tall and reach for it."

"You're obnoxious, you know that?"

Danni relented and went for her purse. Helen pulled it out of range. Danni's arm shot to the right, Helen's hair to the left. This continued until an enormous stretching finger knocked the bag out of Helen's grip. Cathy bounded across the room and snatched it up.

"Keep away! Keep away!" she sang.

A long, slender leg zipped out in front of Cathy and she sprawled out on the floor. The purse flew from her hands and plopped into Kat's lap. Kat was not amused. She set the bag to the side, uninterested in such games.

"Okay," Helen frowned. "I guess that means you're it."

"It?"

"Can you do anything else with your nails other than make them long and sharp?"

"That's about it." Kat said, in her usual monotone.

"So, try something else."

"Like what?"

Helen threw up her arms. "I don't know! We've got a bunch of power tools down here—let's see how tough they are."

Kat didn't budge.

"Be creative. Make shapes with them," Helen prompted. "You like to pick locks. See if you can make one into the shape of a key."

"Or a pizza cutter!" Cathy spurted.

Kat stood. "This is so dumb."

"That's 'cause *you're* dumb." A voice called from the top of the stairs, followed by the thumps of descending footsteps.

With blinding speed, Cathy replaced everything they had disturbed during their practice session. Danni shrank down and grabbed the nearest chair. Helen and Cathy also reverted, no longer glowing, as Lenny's feet tramped into view.

Helen took a step to join the others, but her head jerked backwards, stopping her short. A lock of hair was trapped inside the folded table. She pulled on it a couple of times and when she couldn't get free, she leaned against the wall instead, hiding her blunder from view.

"Lenny!" Cathy's voice squawked. "Leave us alone!"

Her nine-year-old brother continued into the room. He wore a tattered, chocolate-stained T-shirt and muddy shoes he never took off, despite the fact that wearing shoes inside was against the house rules. His curly dark brown hair hung into his face and the telltale Gutiérrez-Guttenberg dimples deepened at the corners of his mischievous smile.

On Cathy, those dimples were endearing. On Lenny, they were downright fiendish. The three Gutiérrez-Guttenberg children shared traits so similar that looking from sibling to sibling was like seeing through a funhouse mirror.

"What are you guys doing in the basement anyway?"

"None of your business! Get out!" Cathy said.

"Catalina, Catalina, Catalina…" he sauntered around the room, his gluttonous eyes probing for something of value. "I was listening to you guys from upstairs."

Helen tried to deflect, wary of this intruder. "Quit being a creep, Lenny."

He was not dissuaded. "What kind of stupid games were you playing down here? Super heroes?"

"Mooooomm!" yelled Cathy

"Oh, for—" Kat caught the little boy around his collar and threatened to punch him, much to the surprise of everyone else. "Are you too afraid to beat up your little brother yourself?"

"You shouldn't do that!" Lenny objected.

"And why not?"

"I'll let her," Cathy said, though Helen doubted she would.

"'Cause I'll tell Mom and Dad you were playing with power tools!"

"We weren't!" Danni's mouth dropped open in protest.

"Then what's Helen hiding behind her back?"

"Nothing, you little brat," Helen said through clenched teeth.

Lenny slipped out of Kat's distracted grasp and stomped back up the stairs, leaving dried pieces of mud in a trail behind him.

"I'm telling Mom!" he cried.

"Telling me what?" Their mother had come to investigate. "What's all this shouting?"

Lenny was quick to yell, "They're down here playing with power tools!"

"Nuh-uh!" Cathy shook her head vehemently as her mom scanned the room.

"Leonardo David, quit being an instigator and leave your sister and her friends alone. They're trying to study."

"But Mamá!"

He always called their mother "Mamá" when he was begging—something Helen had picked up on after she and Cathy became friends. Cathy and Lenny were always at odds with one another, making hanging out together at Cathy's house more of a pain than it was worth some days.

"Don't make me send you to your room!"

As Mrs. Gutiérrez-Guttenberg shooed her son out of the basement, Cathy muttered about her luck.

"Maybe this practice stuff really is good for something."

It was the first time in a long time Helen had seen Cathy's brother get punished instead of her, so Helen let the snide comment slide.

"Did you tell her we were studying?" she asked Cathy.

"No?"

"Well, this has been a blast," Kat said, "but I'm outta here."

No one bothered to stop her as she headed toward the garage door, but she paused by Helen in her uncomfortable position blocking the table. Kat caught a glimpse of Helen's tangled hair and gave a *tsk tsk* as she exited the basement.

"Such a brat," muttered Cathy.

"Which one?" Danni asked, rhetorically.

"On the bright side," Helen said, "good hustle girls!"

Danni frowned. "Coach Calhoun used to say that."

"Will you get over it already? I need help."

Danni crouched next to the folding table to untangle her friend. "Nice one, Helen."

"What's with Kat?" Cathy asked. "She acts like we're so stupid. She used to want to do this. Why can't she make up her mind?"

"We're all taking this a little differently," Helen explained. "Besides, you know what Kat's like. She could be thinking anything."

Helen examined the room to make sure they hadn't missed something in the rush to conceal their secret. "Cathy, I think you spilled our homework on the floor."

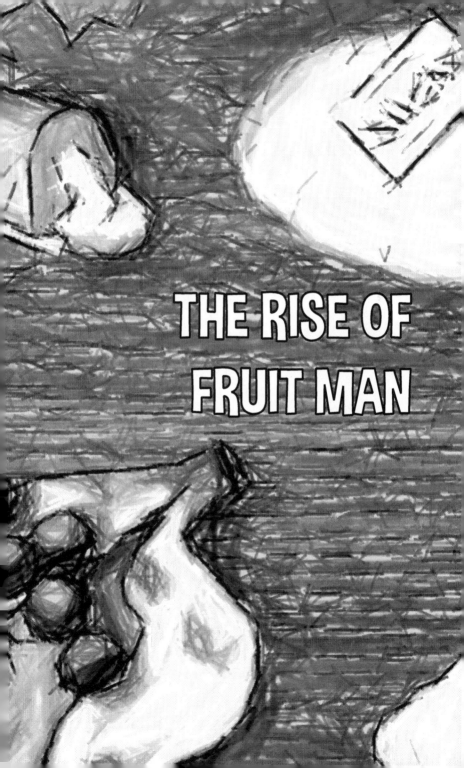

THE RISE OF
FRUIT MAN

Evilspeak (ē'vəl·spēk):

As a mild-mannered person undergoes the changes that lead to villainy, said person develops a phraseology consisting of, but not limited to, monologues, cheesy quips, and a vocabulary filled with large words and alliteration. See also, villainspeak, maniacal laughter.

From Theories on Villain Evolution
Written by Bill

CHAPTER NINETEEN
"Ah, like a true hench-friend..."

Tommy

As more vending machines became crime scenes, the school cracked down on its mysterious thief, though investigations uncovered few clues to help identify the culprit. What fingerprints they found were either smudged and chocolaty, or crystallized and sticky, defying any attempt at identification. The machines were found broken, emptied, and vandalized, with the words "FM Was Here" written in snack cake filling. When warnings and threats failed to deter the culprit, the machines were emptied completely. This affected the entire student body, but none so terribly as the so-called "Fruit Man" himself, Tommy Walker.

Exhausted once again, Tommy was sleeping, visions of sugarplums dancing in his dreams. One kicked him in the leg.

"Go away," Tommy muttered. "The Fruit Man commands you…"

Another poked him in the arm.

"Wake up, man," Zach whispered. "Before Mr. Rombardt sees you."

A hard elbow to the ribs did the trick and Tommy sat up with a start. "What's going on?" he drooled.

"You're sleeping in class. I've been trying to wake you."

"Ah, like a true hench—friend…" Tommy replied wearily. "Zach, my stash is running low and nothing is enough any-more."

"Is class boring you, Tommy?" Mr. Rombardt stopped his science lecture and approached the two students in front of him.

"No, Mr. Rombardt."

The teacher loomed closer. "Really? Then you must be so interested in the dispersal of bryophyte spores that you had to tell Zach what you thought."

"No, Mr. Rombardt."

"Why don't you share your ideas with the class?"

Mr. Rombardt's hand brushed Tommy's as he leaned on the table and a jolt of warm energy surged up Tommy's arm. The teacher stood abruptly, reeling as he reached for his head. He backed away without waiting for a response.

Wide awake now, Tommy kept his eyes on Mr. Rombardt as he retreated to the front of the class and picked up his mug of coffee with a quivering hand. Tommy's new-found alertness had come from something other than his teacher's attempt at humiliation.

The mysterious energy lasted him for the rest of the day, but still, Tommy had trouble concentrating in his classes. What had happened to him in Mr. Rombardt's class? What had happened to Mr. Rombardt? Unlike the fruit that had first fueled him, and the junk food which had energized him later, this was a different, stronger power source. It kept his hunger satiated better and longer. Too distracted for classwork, he tried to determine what his next course of action should be. By the end of the day, Tommy had come to a disturbing conclusion.

Zach met Tommy at his locker, as he had been doing every afternoon for the last couple of weeks. They lived down the street from each other, a fifteen-minute walk from Pearson Middle School. Zach and Tommy had been friends since they were five years old. As Tommy continued to struggle with whatever had been happening to him, Zach had stayed by his side, not allowing him to travel home alone.

Tommy stuffed a heavy book into his bag, still wrestling the raging, screaming cravings in his mind.

"I brought you my half of the candy bars," Zach said, patting his backpack. "You ready to go?"

Tommy softly shut his locker door. The cravings were winning. "There's something I have to do first. Come with me."

Zach trailed his friend away from the lockers. Ever since Tommy's exploit in the cafeteria, he had felt a distance forming between them. Was Zach debating whether or not his best friend still existed? Because Tommy didn't even know the answer to that question. Perhaps a glimmer of hope was what prompted Zach to follow him back to Mr. Rombardt's classroom. Hope, that the old Tommy was still in there somewhere.

Tommy cracked open the door to make sure the teacher was inside. After a quick glance down the hallway, he whispered, "Wait here," and entered the room.

Mr. Rombardt was at his desk, with his feet up, sipping at coffee while he graded papers. He was a strict teacher, but when he noticed Tommy had come into the room, he straightened up to ask if everything was alright.

Tommy's palms were sweaty. He felt his body trembling.

He said nothing as he approached. What was there to say? Tommy wavered one last time, then he leapt onto the desk and grabbed Mr. Rombardt by the head.

"Tommy!" Zach shoved the door open, but froze in place. "Tommy?"

Mr. Rombardt thrashed about, but he couldn't throw the sixth grader. Tommy's eyes were closed tight, as if the strength of their lids was the deciding factor in whether or not he could hold on. He felt a familiar warmth streaming into his fingertips and the out-of-place sweet smell of something caramelizing filled the air. A crackling static throbbed in his ears.

Tommy risked releasing one eye to scan the room. The area where he and his prey grappled had frosted over, even though it wasn't cold. The posters on the walls glazed and cracked around them.

Zach reflexively checked the hallway to see if anyone was coming but had not moved otherwise.

By the time Mr. Rombardt chose to call for help, he had no strength left to do so. With a hand on each side of the teacher's face, Tommy proceeded to drain the life from Mr. Rombardt's body. White-hot energy jolted into his core and every fiber of his being rejoiced. The whiteboard fractured and a piece fell to the floor and shattered. Mr. Rombardt's skin turned grey. His irises rolled back and he trembled.

"Tommy—s-stop," Zach breathed.

Upon hearing his name, Tommy twisted his head around and dropped the teacher to the floor. He rose slowly on top of the desk.

"What did you do?" Zach asked.

Tommy lifted his fists. They were quaking with the raw power now inside him.

"I—I'm—Invincible!" He raised his arms triumphantly, beginning a joyful monologue, "Yasssss! My transformation is complete!" Tommy hopped off the desk and the floor beneath him glazed over in a small radius of rock candy. "I can feel his energy coursing through me! The donut he ate for breakfast, the apple Brittany Jenkins gave him at lunch, the caffeine he has consumed by the gallon on a daily basis since he was eighteen! It is mine, all mine! No longer must I forage for a pittance of pitiful candy bars. No longer must I fear those who would call me little! I am a being of incredible power, and I shall never feel insignificant again!"

Tommy stopped just an arm's length away from Zach, whose back hit the wall. Tommy's eyes had gone white and syrupy goo dripped down his chin.

Zach stuttered, "To-Tommy, you gotta get outta here."

Tommy blinked a few times, coming down from his mania. Was his best friend afraid of him? He wiped some syrup from his cheek and rubbed it between his fingers. He, too, had glazed and frosted over.

"I can't go home, Zach. I—"

Zach stared longingly down the hallway, the only means of his escape. He could run home and forget about this, save himself. Tommy was terrified that he would.

"Please don't leave me," he pleaded.

Zach looked back and forth between the exit and the monster his friend had become.

"We need a place to hide," he said.

Linda

Linda cowered in her chair facing the principal's desk. She had her hands folded together, her trapped fingers shifting this way and that. Her legs were drawn up tightly together, with the tips of her toes just grazing the floor. The principal wiped his lip with an already dampened handkerchief and stared at Linda. Her glasses-magnified gaze returned to him, tenfold.

"Something must be done about these vending machine incidents," he said.

Linda did not respond, but continued to watch her superior without blinking.

"We've had several theories as to who the culprit might be," the principal continued. "Perhaps, it's some ornery little vandals, who think it's fun to steal candy. But then, why wouldn't they also steal the money from the machines?"

Again, Linda did not respond.

"Or perhaps, someone else is doing it. Someone who might have a bone to pick with the administration. Perhaps, someone angry about the food choices offered here at Pearson Middle School?"

Unsure of what to say, Linda continued to lock eyes with the principal's chin, waiting for a clue.

"What I'm trying to say is—ah—Linda, are you this FM? What does it stand for? Have you been destroying the vending machines?"

"Oh…" Linda dropped her head and her gaze fell to her lap.

She thought of the little boy who had begged her for more fruit and how she had refused him, fearing the others would object to so much missing produce. Had she only known the true fate awaiting each apple and pear! Of course, the little boy had gone elsewhere to find the sugar he had said he craved.

"Linda?"

Linda regarded the principal with determination. "I believe I am to blame for the vending machines."

Her statement caused the principal to ease back into his chair as if a burden had been lifted. "No doubt you've heard what happened to Jack Rombardt. With a teacher in the hospital, there is pressure to solve at least one of these crimes."

Shaking with her resolve, Linda forced a bit of strength into her voice, "It is time I told you about the potatoes."

The principal sighed, "Not this again."

"They are changing the students there is a little boy it was my fault!" she blurted

"Stop!" the principal snapped.

His word stabbed Linda to her core and she jolted upright, quieting immediately.

He clenched his jaw and gazed into the bookshelves on the side of the room. Linda could often stare at nothing for hours as her mind worked through meal plans and nutrition estimations, so she recognized the look of someone who was calculating something important. She did not interrupt, listing to his nostrils flare.

The principal sighed and shook his head. "You know Linda, you are not one to let things go, that's for sure." He wiped his forehead, then put the handkerchief away with a note of finality, before folding his hands together over his desk. "The potatoes are just potatoes. A little overprocessed, maybe, but still potatoes. The only 'changes' in the student population will be their test scores. The, ah, company that makes them has assured me that they are chock-full of intelligence boosters for the kids. Doesn't that sound nice?"

Linda felt her head shaking, ever so slightly.

"Just wait until end-of-year testing rolls around! And the good side effect," he continued, "is that they're never ending! We're saving so much from the cafeteria budget."

"Then could we maybe afford—"

"Never mind what we could afford!" the principal snapped. "I'll handle the reallocation of funds."

Linda closed her jaw, swallowing her unasked question. It was neither tasty, nor nutritious. Usually, she couldn't read people very well, but it was clear the principal had no interest in anything she had to say. Her jaw trembled with the effort.

"You've always been a little difficult, Linda, but I never thought I'd have to actually get rid of you."

Linda's jaw positively shook.

"You're not the type to smash into vending machines."

Linda's eyes blurred.

"But your fellow lunch ladies have been coming to me on a daily basis with complaints about your attitude. Your actions have been erratic and you've been described as..." he lifted a sheet of paper from his desk and read, "snippy, suspicious, threatening…" He met her eyes again. "It's only a matter of time before you really are a problem.

"You see, there is much discomfort since this new development. And if you say you are responsible…Well, it's my job to bring order to this vending machine crisis, to calm and comfort the school in this trying time.

"With you gone, the second half of the semester will certainly continue in a calm and orderly fashion."

. . . .

The lunch ladies could barely keep from dancing with glee when Linda passed through the kitchen to collect what few of her belongings she had kept at work. And since they did not care about her absence, they did not care that half of her last produce shipment had mysteriously disappeared overnight.

CHAPTER TWENTY

"So, a little more practice?"

Helen

Helen opened her locker and began sorting through the pile of textbooks and multicolored notebooks at the bottom. Cathy waited, her backpack already heavy with the supplies she was bringing home. The hallways were empty. As usual, Helen's disorganized locker would make her the last to get to her bus.

"So, practice at your house the other night was mostly a success," Helen said.

"I guess."

"I mean, your brother's a real pain, but we have to keep our options open. We can't use my house all the time."

Danni approached them, walking with the typical bounce in her step.

"Did you hear? They fired the lunch lady you two keep talking about."

"The creepy one who's always talking to the food?" Helen asked.

"Yeah," Danni answered. "Word is, she lost it and took it out on the vending machines. Now she's gone, I guess that explains why they're full again."

"I guess." Helen closed the metal door.

"Well, what about Kat's house?" Cathy asked. "We've been there before."

"For practice?" Danni asked. "I'm not sure how welcome we are, you know?"

"Yeah, but we can't exclude her," Helen said. "She's one of us."

Danni waived a dismissive hand. "Whatever you say."

"I'll see if we can use her house this weekend—"

A shriek from somewhere nearby cut Helen off. It stopped short, and an eerie silence followed. Helen's spine stiffened and her heart thudded in her chest. Cathy and Danni were likewise frozen as scuffling noises signaled trouble ahead. Helen's whole body broke out in cold sweat and her mouth was unexpectedly dry.

With a surge of adrenaline, she shouted, "Let's go!"

She spread out her arms and legs to make sure her friends were not too close. Then she concentrated and transformed. The shockwave ripped linoleum tiles from the floor.

Helen bolted toward the attack, leaving Cathy and Danni to stand with their mouths agape.

She rounded the corner and saw a group of figures gathered around one of the newly restocked vending machines at the end of the hallway. They were silhouetted by the afternoon sun coming through the back doors, so she couldn't make out any details yet, but Helen yelled to them in a voice so commanding she even shocked herself.

"Hold it right there!"

Two of the figures jerked up in response. The third dropped to the floor. It was a heavyset girl, who remained unmoving, clutching something in her hands with a death grip. One of her assailants whispered a command to the other and dashed off toward the lockers.

The one who remained stepped forward to intercept Helen and as he approached, his clothing seemed ever more bizarre, made up of different bits of fruit and fruit skin.

He wore a patchwork peel jacket of orange and apple and pear, sewn together with—was it corn silk? Below this colorful assortment were seed-studded peach fuzz pants, which stopped short of a pair of shoes made from the empty rinds of honeydew and cantaloupe. He was ready for action with pineapple shell shoulder, elbow, and knee pads—not unlike a football player who had been hit by a runaway produce truck.

The boy postured in the middle of the hallway, blocking her path. He had a strap of knotted banana peels across his chest, holding a meticulously crafted basket on his back, made from the stems of a thousand cherries. Helen tried to challenge him eye to eye, but she could hardly see them beneath the bunches of grapes woven into his ebony hair.

What face Helen could see was equally puzzled by her own appearance. Even under the florescent lights, Helen's body had a faint, hazy glow about it. Her hair flared like an out-of-control flame in the hallway behind her, and without realizing it, she had manifested a kind of costume onto her person. Sleeveless and dark green, it covered the remainder of her body as a second skin.

With little time to think at all—let alone critique a fashion statement—Helen asked, "Who are you, and what did you do to that girl?"

The boy straightened up and said, "I'm, uh, uh, the Fruity Henchman! And you're, uh, interfering with his plans!"

"His plans?" Helen exclaimed. The poor girl had not moved other than to shiver on the dirty tile floor. "What'd he do to her? It's horrible!"

"He didn't used to be like this—It's just—he needs help!" Fruity Henchman said.

"So does she!"

Helen swiped her hair in a long arc toward her opponent. The henchman dodged and pulled out a fresh slice of juicy watermelon from the cherry stem basket. He slammed it into his mouth.

"Is food seriously all you think about?" Helen asked.

She ran forward, but a sharp sting in the middle of her forehead stopped her in her tracks. Helen felt for a wound, but found a sticky wet spot instead. The Fruity Henchman chewed some more and spat another watermelon seed. It, too, was a direct hit.

"Ew! What is wrong with you?"

The henchman puffed out his cheeks.

Helen's eyes widened. "No way."

He spewed the seeds in rapid succession and Helen ducked and dashed sideways to avoid them.

Pew pew pew!

They ricocheted off the walls and floor, the noise echoing down the hall.

Pew pew pew!

Helen found cover behind a row of lockers, but she couldn't remain there if she wanted to win the fight. He grabbed another slice to reload.

She bolted out from hiding and skittered diagonally to the safety of a library book return box. Seeds pounded against the other side and one nicked her arm. Helen yowled in pain. She jerked in the offended limb, rubbing her elbow to lessen the sting. As she waited for this Fruity Henchman to let up again, Helen saw her friends watching her from the opposite end of the hallway. Safe from the onslaught, there was no sign of action between them.

Helen gritted her teeth, irritated at Cathy and Danni.

She poked her head up when the Fruity Henchman paused to chew. How much watermelon had he managed to cram into his mouth—would there ever be an end?

Helen called to him, "If this is your super power, it's really lame!"

The henchman shifted his seeds to one cheek. "My super power?"

Helen peaked around her cover. "You don't have powers?"

"No."

"Then you're just spitting at me?" Helen scowled. "You're literally just *spitting* at me?"

"…Yes?"

Resolved, Helen jumped out from behind the box and dove underneath a hail of seeds. Before the Fruity Henchman could counteract, she had twined her hair around his shins and pulled him to the floor.

Her opponent fell with a thud. He gulped involuntarily and, rather unpleasantly, his ammunition was gone.

With tiny red welts forming on her arms and face, Helen stood up, her temper seething. Fruity Henchman also stood—not finished, as she had hoped. He reached again into his basket of disgusting goodies.

Red cords of hair waved furiously in his path, but Fruity Henchman ducked and slid past them. He let fly with a volley of soft tomatoes, which splatted against Helen's unprotected suit. Helen swatted at him again with multiple locks of hair.

He put his arms up to block, and Helen was unable to do any damage. It was hair, after all. Frustrated, Helen resolved to work harder on making her hair a more useful weapon.

Of course, it had never occurred to her that she would be fending off flying tomatoes from a mysterious villain's fruit-clad henchman.

In an attempt to make her hair a force to be reckoned with, Helen swung the whole of it around behind her. She planned to thrust it over her head, and down atop her adversary. In her mind, she pictured her hair as a mighty sledgehammer. Fruity Henchman threw his tomatoes at the oncoming mass, in an attempt to stop or slow it, but the hair kept coming.

Until it got caught on an air vent in the ceiling. And two sprinkler nozzles. And a light fixture.

Once again, Helen's hair was stuck.

She pulled and pulled, but her tresses were tangled. Helpless and unable to flee, Helen knew what would come next. She cringed. Fruity Henchman saw his opening and landed one in her face. The acidic tomato innards seared her eyes. As footsteps approached, she swung her arms fiercely, but couldn't yet see friend or foe.

Something grabbed at her arms and Danni's voice called out. "Helen! Helen, calm down!"

When her tears washed the sting away, Fruity Henchman had already fled, and Cathy and Danni had finally come to her aid.

"Gosh, Helen, are you alright?" Cathy asked.

Helen narrowed her eyes. "Just untangle me," she said.

Danni jumped up to pull Helen's hair from the ceiling vent. Each tug pained her scalp and Helen winced, too infuriated with her friends to allow herself a noise.

Cathy pinched a string of tomato goo and pulled it from Helen's suspended hair. "So, a little more practice?"

"A little more help would've been nice!" Helen hissed. She wiped the goo from her cheeks with a downward flourish for emphasis.

"What were we supposed to do?" Danni called back as she carefully freed the last of Helen's locks.

With an angry puff, Helen reverted to normal. "You were supposed to help me catch him!"

"And then what?"

Helen opened her mouth to yell some more, but stopped. "...I don't know."

She slumped to the floor, dejected and disgusting. Helen was covered with slimy tomato which oozed from head to toe. Seeds from the Fruity Henchman's final blow dripped off her chin and into her lap.

"What were you thinking?" asked Danni.

Helen shrugged. "It felt like the right thing to do."

"You look kind of...ick..." said Cathy.

"Check on the girl," Helen whispered, disheartened.

"And what were you wearing?" Danni said.

Helen dropped her head into her hands. "A bodysuit."

"Guys," Cathy beckoned.

Helen and Danni came and hovered over the girl who had been attacked. The area around her had been crystallized. She was frosted in a substance like powdered sugar, which rubbed off on Cathy's palms as she rolled her over. Her ghastly face was stiff and unseeing. If the girl had not been trembling, Helen would have thought she was dead.

"Gross," Helen whispered, clueless about what any of them should do now.

The three recoiled when the girl spoke. "Not like Sean..."

"Wha-what did she say?"

"Not like Sean..." the girl repeated, weakly.

Danni knelt at her side. "It's Tina Hagleman!"

"Can you get up?" Helen asked her.

"Can't move," came the response. "No energy."

Cathy pried the bottle of soda out of Tina's rigid hands. She had evidently bought it from the vending machine before the attack. Cathy unscrewed the cap and poured a little of the caffeinated beverage into Tina's mouth. The shaking diminished and her eyelids fluttered as her pupils came back into focus.

"Danni?" she asked.

"Yeah, Tina. You're safe now," Danni said. "Do you know what happened? Who did this?"

Tina took another sip of the soda. "Don't know...didn't see...He said he needed my sugar."

The girls shared each other's confusion at this odd choice of words.

Helen put a fist to her hip, analyzing the mess. "Whoever it was, it wasn't that lunch lady."

"Wow, you actually saved her," Danni whispered.

"Danni?" Tina reached for her arm.

"Yes?" Danni asked.

"Don't let me end up like my brother. Please? I mean, after what's happened to me, everyone will think I'm gross."

"That's your first concern?" Helen asked.

"No one else saw," Danni told her.

"You won't tell?"

"No, I won't tell."

Tina blinked at her. "You're okay, you know that?"

A door slammed nearby and a squeaky mop bucket rounded the corner. In a panic, the girls scattered, leaving Tina alone in the middle of the powdery, seedy, and tomato-y mess when the janitor appeared.

He bellowed when he reached the scene, grumbling at the chaos he had encountered.

CHAPTER TWENTY-ONE
"There's no turning back after this"

Kat

Kat crouched on her disheveled bed that Saturday, concentrating on the backs of her fingertips. Her nails had been chewed to nubs. It was an unconscious habit—a nasty habit, as Helen had put it—something she did whenever she was nervous. Did other people notice her nail biting? Did she do it that often? She caught herself raising a pinky to her teeth and threw her hand down, pounding it on the mattress.

Why should she feel nervous now, just because she had been thinking about making her index finger into a pizza cutter? Earlier attempts at key making had produced damaged fingernails which bent up into a curlicue so harsh she had to cut it off with scissors when she reverted back to normal.

"Psst."

Kat's head shot up. Her usual cool façade was forgotten, replaced with a flabbergasted gape when she saw Helen's dimly lit face at the corner of the window. Kat glanced to make sure the door to her room was closed before rushing to the frame.

"What are you doing here?"

"You didn't ask her first?" Danni whispered.

Cathy and Danni were huddled behind Helen, shadows in the dusk.

"Can we come in?" asked Helen.

Kat leaned through the window to check the yard, as though she would be scandalized if her neighbors saw the procession outside. She nodded and pulled the curtain away. The three interlopers clambered inside.

Kat's face was an emotionless mask, "This better be the most important matter of life and death—"

"No one answered the front door." Cathy said, dusting herself off.

"—That cities will burn and civilizations will fall. Oceans will overflow and the moon will explode into a ball of fire."

"Ooh dramatic!" Helen said. "But not quite. It's practice time."

Kat glared.

"And that's very important."

At first, the girls took turns working on their faults. Cathy speed-read books so she could be quizzed on their contents. The results had still been disappointing, but she managed to answer one or two questions with a reply having something to do with the subject matter.

Next, they put tangles into Helen's hair and she worked to free herself through force of will. The hair had ideas of its own, and attempted to subdue the tanglers instead. There was much shouting and screaming at Helen for this, but Helen insisted she was not in control.

"Helen! It's tearing apart my room!"

"I can't find Cathy!"

"Make it stop!"

This was all a little too déjà vu for Kat. With a frustrated growl, she grew out her claws to amend the situation. Again. Long red hairs flailed, dropping as they were shorn, until everyone was free from the mess—including Helen. She cried for her lost locks, but was silenced by a unanimous, "Shut up!" in time for them to hear a knock on the door.

"Kat, are you alright in there? What's going on?"

The handle jiggled, and Kat thrust herself against the door to keep it shut. She faced Helen, glowering fiercely.

Helen caught a sob in her throat.

"Nothing's wrong. I've—I've got friends over."

"Friends? But I just got home—wait a minute, are you okay? You don't sound like you."

Kat scowled, mouthing the word, "what?"

She covered her mouth to muffle her voice even better. "I'm not, uh, feeling well...*ahem*."

"Oh, do you—do you need medicine?"

"Whatever, *Mother*."

Her unseen mother exhaled audibly from the other side of the door. "Right. Of course."

Kat put her ear to the door to make sure her mother had gone away.

"Do you always talk to your mom like that?" Cathy asked.

"We could have changed back," Danni offered. "You could have let her in."

"Could I?" snapped Kat, gesturing at the mess.

Even though her mother was gone, Kat could not relax. The heaped masses of sliced red hair had transformed her room into a disaster area.

"Let's just go somewhere else." Kat said.

She waded to the window and climbed outside first.

"It's creepy," Cathy noted from behind. "Your mom—er, mother—didn't think it was your voice. What if, when we're transformed, there's something different about us? Like, if she saw you now, maybe she wouldn't even recognize you."

"That's nothing new," Kat muttered.

She led the way down the street, trying to put the past hour far behind her. Helen was the first to speak up.

"So, Danni, I guess this makes it your turn."

"Maybe we should call it quits," Danni whispered. "Have my mom come pick us up. Those two kids disappeared from this area, you know. They never made it home after school."

"The ones on all the flyers?" Cathy asked.

"Yeah. The police investigated and everything, but still haven't found them."

Kat scoffed. She knew this neighborhood like the back of her hand. There was nothing dangerous on this street.

Helen had paid no attention to the others. "Hey, Danni, could you get so tall you'd be paper thin?"

"What?" Danni asked.

The girls stopped walking, curious at Helen's outlandish request.

"Remember when you transformed in the locker room and you looked all gangly?" Helen continued, "Lately, you've been working in proportion, but maybe you could get that stretchiness back and try being paper thin."

"Um, first of all, ew," Danni said. "But I'd need the length of a football field to do that."

Kat perked up at the thought of making Danni uncomfortable and finally cracked a smile. Within minutes the four of them were in the center of the Pearson Middle School football field. Danni crossed her arms, displeased at this turn of events.

"Fine," she said. "But what good would it be? Unless I had to...what? Fit under some door at the end of a really long hallway?"

Again, Kat smiled.

Danni

"It's easy. All you have to do is stretch out, slip under the door, and unlock it from the inside."

"Just to be clear," Danni said, with craned neck and pursed fingertips. "You're asking me to break into the school!"

"Trust me, you'll love it," Kat insisted

Danni hoped Cathy and Helen, at least, would see the insanity of this plan.

"It's a good idea," Helen said, disappointing her entirely. "We can find out what the school is doing about Tina's attack."

Cathy shrugged, compliant as usual.

Danni snorted. "Fine."

Pressured to perform, she jogged off into the parking lot. "Here goes…"

She planted her feet where they were and stretched towards the front door of the school. It was difficult to keep herself from growing bigger as she elongated. Her head began to throb with the effort, but Danni willed her abdomen and torso to get thinner and thinner as she crawled along the blacktop.

In her mind, she saw blades of grass, reaching for the sky; silken ribbons flowing in the wind. Danni closed her eyes and stretched. She was a strip of cloth, sliding under the foot of a sewing machine; a greeting card, fitting into an envelope. Finally, she was a single piece of paper—a secret love note—slipping silently under the door of the admired.

The grit of the sidewalk scoured her back, and the cool metal of the door frame skimmed along her shoulders. Was she destroying her clothes? Maybe Helen's bodysuit actually made sense.

When Danni opened one eye, an Egyptian-style pictograph across the floor, she saw the ceiling of the entranceway above her. The school was dark and foreboding without the typical daytime hustle and bustle. Nervous bubbles gurgled up in Danni's stomach, but she continued, sliding further into the hallway. She squeezed an arm through what space was left under the door and found the lock.

Danni was extremely aware of her own luminosity in the dark. It wasn't that she and the others were walking, talking glow sticks. She didn't light up the room. It was more like she was covered in reflective material, reacting to a distant light source—as if her body was saying, *look how weird I am!*

So much for being sneaky.

As she twisted the apparatus, Danni's nervous stomach bolted up into her throat. Her hair pricked up on the back of her neck as if someone was watching her. She pushed back the urge to abandon this reckless mission, as her friends were still dead set on the task at hand.

The door creaked as the remainder of Danni's body slithered underneath. Then, Danni opened it to let Cathy, Helen, and Kat inside.

"Have fun?" Kat asked.

Danni ignored her and said instead, "You guys, I think someone's here."

"What?" Cathy asked, hugging herself for comfort.

"The school doesn't have security," Kat said.

"Maybe they do now," Danni argued. "With everything that's been happening."

"Well, we're already here," Helen said. "We should keep going—but stay alert. Which way is the office?"

"How should I know?" Danni hissed.

"This way." Kat said.

Kat led them to the door with the frosted glass window that she had seen a few too many times since the beginning of the school year. The four of them crowded around the menacing doorway with the severe block letters that read:

ADMINISTRATION

"This is it," Helen said. "There's no turning back after this."

"After what?" Cathy exclaimed. "What exactly are we doing here?"

"We're breaking into the principal's office," Kat whispered, using two long fingernails to finagle with the door handle lock.

Cathy clutched Danni's arm. "I wanna turn back."

Danni frowned at Helen.

To reassure them, Helen explained, "We're going to do what the school hasn't. We're going to find out who's been doing these things—vandalizing vending machines, attacking students—and we're going to stop them."

"C'mon, Helen," Danni pleaded. "Who do you think we are?"

"Got it." Kat let the door swing open with a quiet, but eerie creak.

In the darkness, they could see a long, tall desk stretching across the front of the room, with phones and binders spread along its top. Smaller desks were in the corners behind it, and an open doorway loomed in the wall to the right.

"These are the secretaries' desks," Kat whispered, putting a nail into her mouth. It clacked against her teeth and she dropped her hand. "The principal's office is through the next doorway."

The girls dispersed into the room.

"Somebody find a light switch," Helen said.

"No!" exclaimed Danni. "Just in case."

A desk lamp flipped on from the next room, where Kat had gone ahead.

"That'll do." Helen stepped into the office. "Wow, this place is spotless."

"Calm and orderly," muttered Kat.

"Then it should be easy to find what we need and go," Helen said.

Danni sifted through the papers on Principal Pal's desk, while Kat opened the drawers below.

Helen checked the shelves on the side wall, fingering the spines of various binders. "If I was an obsessive-compulsive freak, where would I put investigative documentation?"

"Aha!" Kat grinned. "This night keeps getting better and better."

"Did you find something?"

She was positively beaming. "Yeah. The bullhorn."

CHAPTER TWENTY-TWO

"Juicy Plans"

Cathy

Cathy slid open the drawer of a large filing cabinet. She had hung back while the others entered the principal's office, convinced there was something more important to search for in these rooms. Her friends had given up hope of becoming normal again, but Cathy was still determined to find out where their powers had come from.

Whatever had happened to them had happened within the first week of school. Very likely, it was the day they had all met up in the nurse's office—the first day. She could limit her search to documentation from that date to start. But there was so much paperwork! Finances, personnel, supplies, schedules—the list went on.

Without realizing it, Cathy began speed reading through the filing cabinet drawers.

Helen

"All I can find here are janitorial records," Helen said. "Each of the broken vending machines was documented as a crime, of course, but there's nothing about the mess in the hallway on Friday. I wonder why? Wouldn't that need investigated, too?"

"I found something." Danni picked up a piece of paper from Principal Pal's desk and handed it to Helen. "A limitless, free lunch account under the name Hagleman. At least Tina got something out of this."

Kat shook her head at Danni's naïveté and continued tinkering with the bullhorn, leaving Helen to explain.

"It's a bribe, Danni—to keep her from telling anyone."

"Sounds more like a punishment to me." Kat replaced the bullhorn and moved on to another drawer.

"Why wouldn't the principal want anyone to know about it?" Danni asked.

"Maybe because of this," Helen had found financial folders on another shelf. "He's been cutting the budget to the cafeteria and spending the money somewhere else. It says the money went to the remodel of the teacher's lounge...A Barista 5000, a big screen TV, a leather recliner..."

Kat flipped through the records in the drawer, "Nope. The teacher's lounge doesn't have any of that stuff."

"How would you know?" Helen asked. "You know what, never mind."

Danni had been reading over Helen's shoulder. "What's BMW stand for?"

Helen gasped at the realization. "He's keeping it. Principal Paloski is pocketing the cafeteria budget!"

Kat opened another manila file folder. "Dang."

Helen and Danni stopped what they were doing.

"There is a coverup! Hagleman wasn't the first."

"What?"

Danni and Helen came around the desk so they could see the contents of the folder. Inside, there was information about a teacher who had been hospitalized. The incident form revealed the same post-attack symptoms Tina had shown, but much more severe.

"Why wouldn't he do something about this?" Danni asked. "Call the police or the army or something?"

"Because he doesn't want to get caught." Helen put her hands on her hips, her brow furrowed in thought. *So, the real question is: how are these attacks connected to Principal Pal and the cafeteria?*

"Uh, guys," In the doorway, Cathy held a small stack of gathered papers in her arms. "There's something—"

"Hey! What are you girls doing in here?"

A hunched silhouette had appeared in the doorway and a flashlight shined directly into the intruders' stunned faces. From what Helen could see behind the blinding light, it was an older man with wrinkled, splotchy skin and white hair. His uniform was unmistakable.

"Don't shoot!" Cathy said, throwing her arms in the air.

"Don't be stupid," Kat snapped, pulling her arms down. "It's the janitor."

"Maintenance man." He corrected them in a gravelly voice.

Danni smacked Kat in the arm. "You said there was no security!"

"Ow!" Kat rubbed her bicep. "Technically, I was right."

"What are you doing here?" the man repeated. He put his free hand on his hip, blocking the doorway.

Helen thought fast. "Office cleaning and reorganization as part of the National Junior Honors Society?"

"I doubt that." This new voice did not come from the maintenance man.

Instead, someone jumped him jumped from behind.

"Gah!" He dropped the flashlight when ten small fingers clapped against his head. A pair of little legs wrapped around the man's waist and he staggered backwards through the door.

"It's him!" Helen said.

She and Kat leapt to action. They dashed out to the hallway after the maintenance man and his attacker. Cathy and Danni followed.

The scene was terrifying, but impossible to look away from. The maintenance man twisted and shook. He grabbed at the child on his back, but could not free himself from the attacker's persistent grip. He tried to call out, but hacked and gurgled instead. His energy was draining, and if help didn't arrive soon, there was no telling how far the effects could go.

The attacker's accomplice, who had already been introduced as the Fruity Henchman, blocked the girls' path, a trio of tomatoes at the ready in each hand.

"Stay back, I'm warning you," said the Fruity Henchman.

"Not this time!" Danni's height doubled in an instant and with twice the length of leg, she was able to kick him without even taking a step.

"Nice shot!" Helen exclaimed.

Her team was coming together!

Fruity Henchman fell back onto his rear and slid across the floor, leaving a trail of smeared tomato guts twenty feet down the hallway. He wrapped his arms around his stomach, gulping for air.

"Wow! Sorry!" Danni called.

The smaller boy now stood rigid with power, behind the kneeling custodian. Throbbing light pulsed between the man's body and the outstretched fingers of this new enemy. His eyes glowed, and the corners of his mouth twitched into a wicked smile.

"Hope this works," Kat darted ahead.

Her nails thickened and grew twelve inches. She sliced her hand between their enemy and his victim. Their connection was severed and the maintenance man slumped over, shaking violently.

"No!" the boy yelled. "I wanted more!"

As he reached for his victim again, Helen lurched forward and the entirety of her tresses shot forth, wrapping around the man's waist and pulling him to safety. Kat pulled back to avoid becoming the new target.

"You fools!" the boy shouted. "You melon heads!"

Despite their dangerous predicament, Danni had to stop and whisper, "Did he just call us melon heads?"

"Nobody peels the skin from the juicy plans of Fruit Man!"

"Peels the skin?" Helen asked.

"Juicy plans?" Danni was bewildered.

"Fruit *Man*?" Kat asked. "Is he, like, super short?"

"I thought the other guy was Fruit Man," Danni said.

"No, that's the henchman," Helen explained.

Kat furled her brow. "I'm so confused."

Fruit Man balled his fists and screamed into the air, stirring up a storm of raw sugar energy which frosted the floor and ceiling around him.

"Yeaaaarrrgggh!"

"Helen, I d-don't think this issssuch a good ide-idea," Cathy said from behind her.

"Why? What's he got that we don't?"

"Um, the ability to turn people into limp and trembling useless lumps of candy-coated flesh?" Danni answered, with a gesture toward the maintenance man.

"We have powers, too. It's time we used them," Helen said. "Okay girls, let's take him out. Danni, you pull down some of those ceiling tiles and use them as ammo to distract him. Kat and I will try to subdue him with our nails and hair. Cathy, you—Cathy?"

"Bub-bat guano."

"What?"

Cathy crumpled her collected papers against her chest, vibrating intensely. Her head was twitching.

"Not now, Cathy! Pull it together!"

"Gotta smudge. G-gotta paperclip."

"She's gone," Kat said.

Helen dismissed Cathy for the time being. "Everyone, surround him. Don't let him get a hold of your face."

Fruit Man laughed—an ugly laugh that stopped them dead in their tracks. "What makes you think I have to touch you to drain the energy from you?" He stretched forth his hands like he was palming two invisible dodge balls. "I will quench my thirst. I will have all the power I desire!"

Fruity Henchman crawled to his feet and coughed, "No, Tommy, don't!"

Fruit Man did not heed his friend's pleas. Arcs like wild electricity tore through the air, riding from their source to Fruit

Man's ravenous little fingertips. They flowed through his body, igniting his veins, like lightning strikes across his skin.

A wave of weakness washed over Helen and she dropped to her knees in front of their enemy. Kat and Danni fell to either side of her, as Fruit Man continued to laugh.

"How can three girls contain such reserves of power? I can feel it surging inside me, filling me like an empty drum!"

CHAPTER TWENTY-THREE

"We're Thoomed."

Helen

Fruit Man's laughter died and the glowing energy faded as he stopped his consumption.

"I'm full," he said. "Zach—er, Henchman! Can you believe it? My hunger has finally been abated! I don't think I could absorb more energy if I tried!"

Helen crawled to her feet, patting herself up and down. How was she still conscious? She looked at Danni. "Are you drained?"

Danni had likewise stood and checked herself over. "No"

"I'm not drained." Helen turned to Kat. "Are you drained?"

"I'm good," Kat said. "What just happened?"

"I don't know." Helen whipped her head around. "Cathy! Where's Cathy?"

Cathy's gathered papers lay scattered around her. She had dropped everything she had taken from the office and now twitched and jittered where she stood. Cathy's own power had drawn Fruit Man's attack like a magnet, and she had survived, shaken, but otherwise fine, in the office doorway. Fruit Man had absorbed so much from Cathy that liquid sugar drizzled down his cheeks, seeped from his pores, and pooled around his feet.

"Cathy's sugar high!" exclaimed Danni. "He can't drain her!"

"Can't drain her?" Fruit Man said slowly, then, "Fruity Henchman, my loyal accomplice, seize that girl!"

"But, Tommy," the Fruity Henchman pleaded.

Fruit Man spun around. "Never call me by that little boy's name," he hissed. "I am so much stronger now than I ever was before! I am more! I am Fruit Man!"

"But, Fruit Man—"

"With her, I will have an everlasting supply of the energy I need! The energy to do this!"

Fruit Man threw a fast-hardening glob of white goop which crystallized in midair. Helen, Kat, and Danni each dove aside to avoid getting crushed by the boulder created by their enemy. The rock crashed to the floor with enough force to crack the tile and send candy shards sliding. While the girls were distracted, Fruit Man ordered his accomplice:

"Henchman!" he cried. "Get her now! I'll take care of these three."

Fruity Henchman hesitated. "If I catch her," he asked, "you won't attack people anymore?"

"I can feed off of her for eternity!"

Steeling himself, the Fruity Henchman obeyed. "Okay."

"Stop them!" Helen shouted.

She swept her hair, but the henchman jumped over it with ease. Helen came back again to trip him from behind, but a stream of Fruit Man's goo plastered her hair to the floor. She cried out, exasperated at the familiar tug of stuck hair pulling against her scalp.

"Not again!"

Fruit Man launched another glob towards Helen. It arced upward like it had come from a fountain, and suddenly Danni was there, stopping the projectile with one long arm.

Danni

Danni still wasn't sure that she and her friends should be here, but she also wasn't about to let them get hurt. Not if she could help it. Before the goop could land over Helen's face, Danni had rushed forward to the sound of the meter in her head clicking. She squeaked with disgust, flailing her arm in an attempt to remove the substance even as it solidified around her fist.

"Oh, *now* I get a catch?"

"It's a weapon, you priss!" Kat said. "Use it!"

Yet another stream of slime struck Kat full-on while she was distracted. It slammed her into the entranceway's bulletin board, displayed like yesterday's old news, next to a set of flyers for the two missing students. Little more than her head was visible above the splatter. The sugar crystallized around her, pressing in on her, impervious to her struggles.

Danni swung her giant fist into the ground, quaking the metal lockers that lined the hallways. This was no log in the forest—She could wield true power here, with her size and its proportional strength. *Maybe I should start doing pushups*, she thought.

She swung again, sideways this time. Fruit Man hopped backwards to dodge and Danni spun around with the force of her heavy fist's momentum. She struck a wall, which cracked the sugar around her arm, freeing it for regular use. She lunged at Fruit Man, but he sidestepped and she slipped on a puddle of slime that he had left for her. Danni fell face first, hitting her chin on the floor. A sharp pain jolted inside her mouth.

Seizing his opportunity, Fruit Man aimed at the ceiling and shot goo until the tiles above were too heavy to remain aloft. Chunks mixed materials came crashing down on top of Danni. Another *click*, and her body rolled to the side, but not fast enough to save her legs from the falling debris. Danni strained, but what had fallen on top of her had fused together, too weighty to budge. *Definitely will be doing pushups,* she decided.

Cathy

Cathy saw the action taking place around her, but couldn't find a rational idea within her mind to act on. She stammered, "F-fuzzy caterpillars—gotta flit—" as Fruity Henchman stalked towards her.

Having exhibited none of her abilities thus far, Cathy seemed of little threat to Fruity Henchman and as he closed in, Cathy finally willed her legs to move. She turned to run—and rammed herself into a wall. Her brilliant escape attempt was therefore thwarted by Fruity Henchman, who was able to stroll up and apprehend her.

He smelled *very* ripe.

When Fruit Man saw that all had gone in his favor, he advanced on Cathy and her captor. "All this battle! I believe it's time to recharge already."

"No!" Helen scrambled to her feet and ran at him, the length of her hair increasing fast enough for her to reach him.

Cathy watched as Fruit Man fired another staple of goop into the red locks, catching them in a second place. Helen's feet kept going, but her head yanked her back. She thumped to the floor, flat on her back, reaching for her tailbone.

She hissed. "Aaahhh...maaan..."

Fruit Man put a hand over Helen's shoulder and she caught her breath.

"I don't need you," he said.

Instantaneously crusting gunk spilled over Helen's chest and she was bolted in place.

For Cathy, claustrophobia was setting in. She found she did not like being forced to stay still. Staying still gave her the jitters. The jitters gave her the shakes. The shakes gave her the tremors. The tremors gave her enough freakish momentum that Fruity Henchman couldn't keep his arms around her. Her mind was flying—*Carwash, apples, sneaky, centipedes*—She couldn't keep anything still. Fruity Henchman shuddered with Cathy as he tried to keep her contained. His crafty clothing was falling apart at the seams.

"Ah, my arms!" he said through gritted teeth, as the friction intensified.

"Horseshoes!"

With a yelp, the Fruity Henchman released his prisoner.

"You won't escape so easily from me!" Fruit man raised his arms, preparing to detain Cathy as he had the others.

"I gotta, uh…" she tapped her toes and shuffled her feet. Cathy considered her friends—plastered, bolted, and buried. "I gotta…"

"Run!" someone yelled.

"Run, Cathy!"

"*Run!*"

Cathy took a deep breath. She shrugged at Fruit Man and his henchman. "I gotta run."

She disappeared down the hall.

Helen

Fruit Man blinked, and his prey was gone. "After her!" he ordered.

They chased after Cathy on her psychotic scurry, leaving her friends alone in the darkened hallway.

Helen whistled, impressed. "That was fast." She tugged at her hair to get a look at her comrades. "Are you okay, Danni?"

"I bit my thung."

"Kat?"

"Shut up."

"I'll take that as a yes."

Danni clenched her teeth and pushed with all her might, but her might did little against the world's largest chunk of rock candy. "If I thrink, ith'll cruth me. I'm thtuck."

"Me too." Helen gave her neck muscles a rest and laid her head on the floor. "I guess there's nothing we can do, but wait for Cathy to singlehandedly defeat two enemies and come to our rescue."

"We're thoomed."

Distant noises arose from the schoolwide chase, but in the silence of the middle school's sugarcoated entranceway, there was only a faint scratching.

"What's that sound?" Helen asked, rolling her eyes up to see over her forehead.

The scratching was followed by a crumple, and one of Kat's nails began to cut through the rock that bound her.

CHAPTER TWENTY-FOUR

"Time to flee strategically"

Cathy

Cathy felt better now. This brisk jog was helping to clear her head. Tile and carpet blurred alternately under her feet. Gee, her legs were moving fast. She looked up and there was a door.

Door!

Cathy plowed through the door, slamming it open and summersaulting onto the classroom carpet. Cathy sprung to her feet and she resumed her exercise. Why was she running again?

Two pairs of arms swiped by her as she exited the room.

Oh, yeah!

She could have fun with these two.

The next thing Cathy knew, she was running on the ceiling. Of course, that would be impossible.

But what did ol' Fig Newton *really* know about gravity, anyway? The proof of her act was in the uprooted ceiling tiles, cascading onto the heads of her pursuers.

Better not tempt Mother Nature, Cathy thought.

She jumped back up, onto the ground and zipped away. How did she end up in the library? When she snuck a peep backward, to see if she was still being followed, she hit a bookcase.

It tipped and fell against another bookcase.

In a domino effect, a row of shelves collapsed, littering the library with fallen books.

She wrinkled her nose. This wouldn't do. Books were precious commodities. She couldn't let them remain on the floor like trash.

Fruit Man and his Fruity Henchman stood in the middle of the library, getting dizzy as Cathy looped circles around them, putting the books away. Her friends were probably worried about her. She decided she should head back soon.

Maybe she could glue herself to the wall so they wouldn't be lonely.

Kat

With an upward sweep of her arm, Kat broke the left half of her body free. Scored up pieces of her sugar prison dropped and shattered as she jammed her claws into what remained of Fruit Man's sticky trap. She pounded at it with her fist. When

Kat tumbled away from the wall, the remaining chunks that had surrounded her fell and slid over the tile like ice. She gathered herself, suppressing the fury welling up inside her.

Kat stomped to where Helen lay on the floor. Her lips were curled in a goofy smile.

"You freed yourself! If I didn't know better, I'd say you've been—"

Kat sliced a set of two-foot-long nails across the ground, cutting Helen free. Helen shuddered at how close the blades had come to her face.

Kat had no patience for Helen and her ill-timed sense of humor. In a few rage-fueled seconds, she had Helen's hair free. A crash from within the library made her flinch. Cathy's useless and disruptive behavior would be the end of them, for sure.

They went to help Danni next. Helen grunted as she strove to work her hair like a car jack underneath the slab of crystallized ceiling that pinned Danni to the floor.

"There's not enough rigidity in hair for it to prop up something so cumbersome."

Kat scoffed and willed her nails to cover her fingers, ice pick style. Right now, she didn't want to study the vocabulary list Cathy and Helen kept throwing in her face.

"There'th goo thlipping down my neck," Danni whined.

Kat jammed her picks into the crystal. She hated helping someone so prissy, and to top it off, she hated this. All of this. As large, but more manageable, chunks of sugar broke away,

Helen tossed them aside, giving Danni the chance to wiggle herself free.

Shrinking down to her normal size, she slurred, "Thankth, guyth."

The three girls jerked back as an arc of goop struck a set of entranceway doors, sealing them shut.

"They're trying to lock us in!" said Helen.

A giggling blur shot through the entranceway and back into the school.

"No!" Danni exclaimed. "They're thtill chathing Cathy!"

The bungling villains stumbled through the mouth of the hallway, but they changed course as Cathy dashed past them again. She had been preceded by an aimless chain of watermelon seeds and pursued by Fruit Man and henchman, who skidded into the open as they changed course mid-run.

"Cathy!" Helen shouted.

"Oh, hi!" Cathy reappeared and disappeared once again.

"Stop! Come back!"

"Can't," she said as she blew by.

"Danni, stop her. Kat, get ready."

Kat crouched. *Ready for what?* Did Helen even have a plan at this point?

The next time Cathy streaked through, Danni snatched her with waiting arms. Cathy's momentum kept them both moving for another thirty feet and Danni's abdomen stretched out as she was pulled across the empty cafeteria. Danni pressed her heels against the tile and clenched her muscles, slowing the psychotic speedster as they reached the end of the room. Cathy plopped down on the floor, content.

Helen zipped her hair across the hallway and Fruit Man and Fruity Henchman came lurching over its top. They sprang to their feet and Fruit Man scanned the room, seeing that his enemies had managed to escape their various snares.

Kat's fingertips tingled. They had already been defeated once by this menace, and she had no confidence they could survive a second attempt. Poised and tensed, she waited for the attack to commence once again. Danni remained crouched next to Cathy, and Helen stood ready at Kat's side. The Fruity Henchman pulled a couple of tomatoes from his basket, but Fruit Man stopped him.

"I have drained enough energy to last a while, but fighting again will deplete me of my reserves. Now is the time to flee strategically," said Fruit Man. "Pick up those papers."

Cathy hiccupped.

As their foe was about to escape, Helen shouted, "He's getting away!"

Fruit Man put up his hands and a thick wall of rock-hard sugar formed a frame around them. It multiplied in on itself, enclosing the hallway and blocking the villains from their view. Kat rushed forward, side by side with Helen's growing hair. The long train of hair passed her up and wrapped itself around the waist of the fallen maintenance man, lying forgotten at the edge of the hallway. She sucked him under in the nick of time, before the wall of sugar closed.

Kat scratched at the wall with long, frantic swipes, but it was clear she would never break through the crystal-like barrier in time.

She snapped at Helen, "Why didn't you grab Fruit Man?"

"I-" Helen stammered, "I didn't think about it."

Helen's disappointment was clear on her face. Cathy sat calmly on the floor, and Danni was obviously relieved.

"We suck at this!" Kat yelled.

Everyone flinched when she turned her wrath on the wall and slammed her fists into it once again.

"I'm going home."

Helen

Kat stormed through the school's front doors and vanished alone into the night. Her friends remained, hanging their heads.

Helen clenched her jaw and willed her eyes to suck the tears back in. She couldn't let them fall, not while the others could see. What had just happened to them was too serious—too dangerous for her to even comprehend yet. She had pushed her friends into doing this, had endangered them.

No, it was worse than that. She had nearly cost them their lives again. Helen surveyed the damage they had caused to the school. They had been lucky to survive with nothing worse than bumps and bruises. Helen sniffed and turned her face away from her friends as the dams on her lower lids began to break.

"We have to go," Danni whispered. "We can't thtay here."

Danni

Danni was grappling with her own anxiety. She was bruised all over from a fallen ceiling! For once, her worst fears had come true. The school had literally caved in around her, but she had survived and surprised herself. Things had gotten way out of hand, but she had fought for her friends, and she was proud of it. This was so much bigger than anything happening to Priscilla and her gaggle, with Danni right in the middle of everything!

The school was dark and foreboding once again, with two dangerous enemies lurking somewhere within. She sought her comfort from Cathy, but all she got was hiccups.

"Papers." *Hiccup!* "Potatoes."

"What?" she asked.

"Papers." *Hiccup!* "Potatoes!"

"Tell us later," Helen said. She sniffed once. "Let's get out of here."

They lingered at the front of the school until they heard sirens coming. They had reverted and called an ambulance for the maintenance man, but there were extra sirens—a whole convoy of flashing vehicles. Danni puffed at her inhaler, and the three limped away to avoid the authorities.

Kat

Kat ran back through the football field, wiping her eyes violently with the backs of her arms. She tore at her own fingernails when they wouldn't shrink fast enough as she traveled back to the sanctuary of her room.

But she stopped and fell to her knees when she remembered her sanctuary had been torn apart by the others earlier that evening. She hated them. She sobbed. She hated them!

She had been begging for this to work. So desperate to have found something she could belong to. So desperate for friends she could keep. But it hadn't worked. She hated Fruit Man and his stupid henchman for making a fool out of her. She hated how it felt to risk everything and lose.

She hated Helen for making her want to laugh. She hated Cathy for being crazy and brilliant at the same time. She hated Danni for always caring for her friends. Kat didn't want to like them. She wasn't supposed to. She was an outsider and the four of them made no sense together.

Kat wheezed and dug into her pocket for her inhaler.

They made everything change. Was she supposed to change with them? All this was because of them and Kat hated them for it. She hated not knowing which direction to turn.

CHAPTER TWENTY-FIVE
"That couldn't have gone any better"

Kat

Monday morning, the school was still in disrepair, with orange cones and caution tape around the messes. Principal Paloski appeared at lunch to rationalize the situation to the gathered students, who had already made up their own rumors. He climbed the platform at the end of the cafeteria and raised his arms to quiet everyone. When shouting and waving failed to gain the students' attention, he pulled the trigger on his beloved megaphone.

MOOOOOO!

The cafeteria hushed. Principal Pal stared at the contraption, just as confused as the students around him.

MOOOOOO!

"What in the—" He shook the bullhorn and smacked the battery pack with his palm. "Someone has sabotaged my megaphone!"

Kat leaned back with her arms crossed and a smug upturn at the corners of her lips. "Worth it."

MOOOOOO!

The student body was hysteric.

"Alright, alright, that's enough. Calm down," he called. As the laughter died away, he continued. Shouting without the help of the device, he said, "You may have noticed some construction around the school, in the library, and the entranceway. Rest assured, there is nothing to worry about. We are making improvements for your benefit…"

"Pft." Kat swiveled around to put her chin on her hands, ignoring the rest of the principal's speech. Instead, she directed her attention to Cathy's meal.

The lunch tray was in the middle of the table, its contents cold and stale. Upon this lunch tray sat a pile of mushy peas, a hot dog of sorts; and a giant, congealed, whitish, speckled mound of gravy-covered mashed potatoes—that lied.

They had been discovered for what they truly were—an engineered imitation, a disgrace to the true and beloved side dish of home-cooked family dinners. Yes, an abnormal disaster had been splotched atop this tray, coated in its gravy juices, neutralized against whatever fantastic effects it could have on any who consumed it.

"The gravy is the key," Cathy whispered to Helen and Kat. "According to the files I read last night, it's a special recipe to activate mental acuity and neutralize any 'harmful reactions' that might build up within the potatoes."

Leaning gloomily on the table, Kat stewed in her discomfort. This weekend had been mentally and physically exhausting. Even more so for Kat, who had spent an extra hour of her night stuffing trash bags with piles of hair and sneaking them into garbage cans all around the neighborhood.

Cathy and Helen had come to the lunch table lacking their usual banter. Kat had given them no welcome, glaring especially hard at Helen. Kat didn't have to sit at this table. She didn't have to show up at all. But here she was, uneager to discuss what had happened that weekend.

On the other hand, Cathy was bursting at the seams, telling them she had important information, which could be the key to solving their problems. She was a genius, a savior, her very own knight in shining armor, herself. This was the most clearheaded and focused that Kat had seen her. She hadn't been able to wait for Danni to relate what she had learned.

Helen, for a change, was silent.

Principal Pal said something about order and calmness as he finished his announcement and retreated from the stage. The cafeteria resumed its usual volume.

"Now, it didn't say what kind of reactions, or from what. At least, it wasn't specific. Something about the process through which the potatoes were prepared. You see, they weren't made here. Hardly anything is." Cathy furrowed her brow as she re-accessed the information she had gathered the night before. "But the potatoes go through some *undisclosed* procedures during harvest and mashing. There were warnings and disclaimers all over the paperwork."

Drawn into Cathy's explanation, Kat asked, "Why would they serve something like this in a school lunch?" She fixated on the principal's back as he schmoozed his way through the cafeteria.

"It's cheap," Cathy explained. "And, because of its chemical-genetic makeup, it's been classified as meat, fruit, vegetable, dairy, *and* grain! Haven't you noticed they've been serving potatoes with every meal?"

"Wait a minute. This is just nuts." Kat jammed her fingers in her hair as she pieced everything together. "Helen, why aren't you saying anything?"

Cathy elbowed her friend, and Helen's vacant stare faded. She lifted her head, mumbling "origin story" under her breath, and she blinked back and forth between them.

"Huh?"

"Helen, the potatoes?"

"Uh, yeah! That's wack."

"Wack?" Kat said. "*Wack?* Have you even been listening to Cathy?"

"Sorry. I was—"

"She just told us we've been mutated from eating this stupid school's radioactive GMO potatoes!"

"Uh, not quite—" Cathy said.

Helen piped up. "I'd hardly say they were radioactive. If they were radioactive, we'd glow or something," she said.

Kat and Cathy said nothing.

"Oh, I suppose we do glow a little." After a beat, Helen continued, "But come on. You're both treating this like it's a bad thing."

Kat slapped her palms on the table. "What?"

"Hi guys." Danni dropped her lunch and took her seat.

"Where've you been?" asked Cathy.

Before Danni could open her mouth, Kat answered for her. "Where do you think? She was chatting it up with the rest of Priscilla Driscalle's gaggle, worming her way in, like the insect she is!"

Danni gasped.

"I guess that'd make her a glow worm?" Helen's joke and finger guns were lost on their audience.

"Don't you see?" Kat raised her voice. "You're a stepping stone to her. The minute she's allowed at that table, she'll abandon you, just like—like—" she faltered. "Why don't you quit trying to be someone else?"

This time, Danni snapped back at her. "Look at you, giving people advice. Maybe you should just pick who you are and be it!"

Kat stood. "Fine."

She scooped her belongings into her open backpack and stormed off toward the familiar round table where Jason, Ben, and Miranda sat, waiting.

Helen

Helen crossed her arms. "Well, that couldn't have gone any better."

Danni wheeled around on Helen. "This isn't the time to be funny. Sometimes sarcasm isn't appropriate!"

"Are you kidding? I would be hard-pressed to—"

"I mean it, Helen!"

Helen threw her arms into the air. "Whadaya want? It's who I am!"

"Yeah, well, we get the idea."

"Oh, do you?" Helen shouted. "Maybe Kat isn't so wrong about you!"

"What? Because I don't find you funny right now?" Danni thrust her finger in Kat's direction. "She doesn't even know who she is!"

"Thanks to you, she does, now!" said Helen.

"Oh, everything's a joke! Maybe you should quit trying so hard to be yourself," Danni retorted.

The girls' voices had raised to the point that two of the lunch room attendants were moving in their direction.

"That's the dumbest thing I've ever heard!" Helen said.

"Is that so? Sorry I don't get your sophisticated humor. Am I not good enough to hang out with anymore?"

"Apparently, *I'm* not! Why do you want to sit with them so much?"

"What's wrong with expanding your group of friends?"

"Because you're better than them! Can't you be happy with what you've got?"

A lunch room attendant stalked up to each side of the table. Helen and Danni were told to sit down and stop shouting, at the threat of getting moved to opposite sides of the room. When faced with actual separation, the girls obeyed, but they kept their backs to one another. Across the lunch room, Helen saw Kat and her darkly clad friend, Miranda, exchanging a small bottle of black nail polish. Priscilla and her friends tittered about the commotion and pointed at Danni.

The lunch table was emptier without Kat's presence, stony though it may have been, and that emptiness was amplified by the silence and lack of camaraderie. They had shared a dangerous misadventure and the information Cathy had relayed to them was earthshattering. Everyone was on edge and Helen couldn't let one regretful argument break up their friendship. They needed each other now.

"I'm sorry, Danni. Sorry for always saying funny things when, maybe I shouldn't. Sometimes, I just don't know what else to say. It's just…easier to make jokes."

Danni turned around to accept her apology, "I was checking on Tina. I'm sorry if you guys think I'd rather be over there all the time."

"I know," Helen added, "No one should tell anyone who they can and can't be."

"Yeah," Danni cast a regretful glance in Kat's direction.

Quietly, Cathy said, "What if you don't like who you are?" This was a drastic change from the bubbly, talkative person she had been moments ago. "You guys are defending your personalities, and I don't even have one."

"That's crazy!" Helen said.

"Yeah," Danni added. "You've got a great personality. You're smart. You're nice."

"You never have anything mean to say," finished Helen. "And you're super dependable. There's no one I can count on more than you, Cathy."

Cathy's lips curved a weak smile.

"You found out about the potatoes," Helen continued.

"Potatoes?" Danni asked.

"Yeah, I guess."

"And you've got the best taste in friends," Helen added.

Danni rolled her eyes and the girls basked in the reaffirmation of their friendship.

With renewed excitement, Cathy said, "But now that we know the potatoes caused this, we can work on finding a cure!"

"The potatoes? Really?" Danni asked.

"No," Helen said. "Not until Fruit Man is taken care of."

"You're kidding me!" Cathy's whole body sagged as her gloominess reemerged.

Likewise appalled, Danni asked, "How could you even suggest going back for more? He beat us last time."

"Not entirely."

"But we lost. Like, definitely, we lost."

Helen brought her hands together and bowed her head as she worked through the facts. "He's gotta be a potato freak," she told her friends. "Like us."

"Freak?" Danni whimpered.

"The boy from the lunch line!" Cathy said.

"And it's obvious no one else in this school can stop him."

"They are just covering it up," Danni reluctantly agreed.

"Then it's up to us. Whether we like it or not, we're the only ones who even stand a chance."

"So, what do we do?" asked Danni.

"We may have lost last time," Helen said, "but we learned how he fights. We saw what he can do. Using that information, we can practice harder—find new ways to use our powers. We'll work on our flaws." To reassure them, she added, "Next time, it'll be different. I promise."

"But when is next time? How long until we run into him again?" Danni asked.

"Not long," Cathy said.

"What? What do you mean?"

"He knows." Cathy's voice was grave. "He stole the papers I was reading that night. He knows the school's behind it. He knows they're covering it up. What if he gets mad? What if he wants revenge?"

"Then we have to work fast." Helen said. "We need to be ready to stop him."

It is not possible for a person to learn everything there is to learn (believe me, I've tried), but as our brains take in knowledge, they come to certain conclusions about the world around them—in this case, specifically, its rules. When impossible things are seen, the body freezes while all functions are diverted to the mind and its search for explanation. Hence, the jaw-dropped, wide-eyed appearance of the surprised (see also, Bill's *Anatomy of the Ultimate Prank*). When something as incredibly impossible as the girls' transformation is witnessed, the mind simply refuses to recognize it as truth.

While the eyes are still registering the image before them, the brain continues disbelieving, forcing a rift between the information that is gathered and that which is comprehended. This rift is identified by a distortion in the vision of the perceiver. Once recognized objects are undetectable, overshadowed by the unrecognized truths the mind is grappling with realizing. This anomaly forms a crisp barrier to the world around it, appearing as aberrant illumination, a fuzziness, an "aura of unreality," if you will. Therefore, no one originally recognized these girls once they had transformed, even having transformed in full view of others. Due to this "aura of unreality," the true identities of Catalina Gutiérrez-Guttenberg, Helen Hughes, Katherine Crenshaw, and Danielle Emerson remained secret for quite some time.

From "Complexities of Transformation,"
a chapter in *Research in ST Pseudosciences*

CHAPTER TWENTY-SIX

"This is it"

Linda

Almost two weeks had passed since the principal had relieved Linda of her kitchen duties. Now, she arrived back at the school to ask the too-much-lipsticked-one, her former supervisor, if she could use her as a job reference. Linda had expected to enter a peaceful kitchen, with quietly humming machinery. The three still-employed lunch ladies should have started to microwave their various food products in preparation for the lunch hours. Linda paced outside, and eventually pushed on the loading door buzzer.

Receiving no answer, she tried a couple more times, then she slid open the door and crept inside. When she reached the kitchen, it was eerily quiet and she could see no one at work.

"Hello?" she ventured. "Lunch women?"

There was no reply.

"Can I use you as references?"

A tumultuous crash from the storage room caused her to jump. Linda tiptoed in that direction, and when she came upon the familiar metal shelving and stacks of food-product boxes, she found her three former coworkers hovering around a mess of spilled plastic lunch trays. As the tallest of the lunch ladies, it had been Linda's job to do anything involving the top shelves.

The ladies looked up, shocked to see Linda standing in front of them. Shocked, and terrified. It had never occurred to her that getting fired for lunacy and acts of violence meant she was not allowed back on school grounds.

The three ladies screamed in unison.

Linda screamed back in surprise.

The lunch ladies screamed some more.

Linda screamed, too, but this time in reaction to the glowing beams of light which burst out from the three women. Linda panned her head, following the beams to their destination.

Surrounded by eerie luminosity, a child's figure levitated and received the energy drawn from Linda's former coworkers. A clear, viscous slime dripped and pooled on the floor beneath him and he laughed maniacally.

The figure landed and the three lunch ladies hit the ground; *clunk, clunk, clunk*. Their bodies were frozen in their startled positions, faces twisted with horror.

A voice from the figure: "Ahhhh. That was refreshing."

At first, all Linda could see were his glowing white eyes. But, as the aura of light around him faded, she recognized the little boy who had taken the tray of non-neutralized generic mashed potatoes that lied—the little boy to whom she had once slipped stolen fruit—the little boy she eventually let down. But he was no longer a little boy. Now, he was nothing but energy— sugars, corn syrup, caffeine, and refined carbs—everything that Linda hated contained in one frightening, angry little lump, covered with goo.

Linda pointed a quivering finger toward the walk-in refrigerator. "You can have all the fruit they don't use it."

The little boy cackled, and as he did so, Linda sensed the wafting odor of the rotten-fruit child next to him.

Her lower jaw shuddering, Linda spurted, "Could you turn them back please? They weren't that bad."

His lips were twisted in a slick, slimy sneer. "Don't worry, I won't do that to you."

"Okay."

"After all, you made me the Fruit Man."

Linda trembled. She had not a clue what she was supposed to do now. Shouldn't an adult be able to tell a little boy to stop crystallizing people? But she only had experience conversing with fruit. She didn't particularly like sugar.

"Orange you glad?" said the little boy. "You get to witness the destruction of the school, firsthand."

1

Linda said nothing. The other child said nothing.

The little boy coughed. "*Ahem.* Zach, we've discussed this."

The rotten-fruit child jumped. "Huh? Oh! Y-yeah, that's just peachy...boss."

The little boy loomed maliciously. He held up a wrinkled and crusty school document. "Now, tell me where to find these mashed potatoes."

Danni

"So, who else slept last night?" Helen asked.

Cathy blinked one long, slow blink.

Danni wobbled her hand in a so-so response.

The girls had had a fretful and grueling week of honing their abilities and they were still piecing together a plan of action. The truth was, Danni hadn't slept a wink. But she put on a brave face for her friends.

"We know he hates being called 'little,'" Helen continued. "We can use that to our advantage. Maybe if we make fun of him, he'll get mad and make mistakes."

Danni yawned. "We've been over this a thousand times. Can't we stop for, like, a minute?"

"Not if we want to beat him."

"But how? We don't even know who he is," said Danni. "He could be anybody. If we could catch him at a time when he's not using his powers, that'd be something."

"But we do know who he is."

Helen laid a couple sheets of paper on the table. Torn down flyers of the two missing boys had been crudely drawn over with crayon. One Zachary Park had purple orbs colored over his hair and blocky tropical shoulder pads beneath his face. The other, a Tommy Walker, had his eyes whited out and eyebrows redrawn into an angry scowl.

Danni stared at the papers. Exhaustion blurred her vision and really brought the drawings to life. "Well, that makes too much sense."

"I don't think he can hide the way we can," Cathy said. "Now that I know what to look for, I see signs of him everywhere, like he's been living in the school."

She pointed.

The maintenance man grumbled and snarled as he jabbed a broom handle at a crystalline formation pouring out of a ceiling vent.

"Yeck." Helen cringed. "Glad old Murphy's okay, though."

When a chunk eventually broke off, Murphy paused to catch his breath with his broom across his knees.

"Well, mostly okay."

Danni sighed. "At least we already know how to break into the school."

Helen had her head propped up on her elbows. "Stop jittering, Cathy, I'm trying to concentrate and you're shaking the table."

"Uh, that's not me."

As the vibrations got worse, Danni put her hands up to quiet her friends. "Wait. Do you hear that?"

The cafeteria had gone silent as more students noticed the distant rumble. The lunch aides tried to calm everyone while hiding their own trepidation. Principal Pal had even come out of his office, searching for the source of the noise.

The children who had gone up to purchase food came running and screaming from the lunch line. Heeding no objection from the adults, they made a beeline for the doors. All heads turned from the fleeing students to face the kitchen as a pulpy white sludge erupted from the doorway and consumed the nearest table. The stillness shattered, replaced with absolute chaos as students ran for safety. Someone hit the fire alarm.

The cafeteria had emptied by the time the rolling white mounds of over-rehydrated mashed potatoes reached the second lunch table. Screams resonated through the middle school as the entire population of Pearson evacuated. Principal Pal paced ahead of the deadly mass, waving his useless megaphone and shouting for the students to remain calm and to exit the building in "an orderly fashion."

The conquering spuds growled into a massive upheaval that Principal Pal never saw coming. He was swallowed whole, engulfed bullhorn and all, by a potato tsunami, which crashed into the next set of lunch tables. Needless to say, the situation was grim.

Danni, Cathy, and Helen watched together as the danger escalated.

"This is it," Helen said. "This is what we've been prepping for."

Cathy shook her head. "I don't remember anything about potato tidal waves."

"It has to be Fruit Man," Danni said. "No one else would do something this twisted and sick."

"Alright." Helen surveyed the cafeteria. "This way is blocked, but if we go around, maybe we can get to the source and stop it."

The girls left the cafeteria, running the long way, toward the elective classrooms. It was their only route, to battle their enemy again, to what could become their final defeat. The girls moved bravely forward. The entire school was filled with the low, gurgling grumble of steadily growing mashed potato product. Through the din, Danni caught the words of a particular group of students as they rushed to get out of the school.

"C'mon, Kat, let's get out of here. I know somewhere we can ditch the rest of the day."

"Yeah, Kat, let's go."

Kat was with her new friends, watching as the others raced toward the danger. Danni stopped and went to her. She was wearing black lipstick and nail polish to match the Morlocks. The makeup contrasted harshly against her pale skin. Kat's eyes darted back and forth between the cafeteria and Danni's face.

The tallest of her friends chuffed. "Another weird friend of yours?"

"Weird?" Danni jerked back. *Coming from this guy?*

"OMG!" the short girl said in a mocking voice, "She, like, totally wants to do your hair and makeup, Kat."

"Shut up, Miranda." The third Morlock grabbed the arm of the tallest, "Let's just go, Jase."

The group started to leave, but Kat didn't budge.

"Listen," Danni said, "I know what it's like to want to belong to something, but you already do, Kat. This stuff that's happened to us…We can't run from it or pretend it isn't there, because it's inside us. Whether we want it or not, it's part of us. And no one else could understand. I guess, all we have is each other. And with these powers…like Helen said, it feels like the right thing to do."

She gave Kat a weak smile before sprinting away to catch up to Cathy and Helen. She heard the tall Morlock's voice as she ran away.

"Look, Kat. That dumb friend of yours is such a loser— she's even running the wrong way."

CHAPTER TWENTY-SEVEN

"No, you touch him!"

Helen

As the three rounded the corner, the sloppy wet slapping sound of the potatoes grew much more intense. The mounds of generic food poured forth from the far kitchen door, but the nearest one remained unobstructed.

"Look!" Helen shouted. "We're in luck."

Danni turned to her. "Define 'luck.'"

"So, who's first?" Cathy asked.

"I'm the leader. I guess I should go," said Helen.

Danni objected. "Hey, wait a minute! When did we decide that?"

"It just seemed obvious."

"Maybe to you! But to us sane people—"

"Uh, guys…" Cathy said.

"What makes you think you've got what it takes?"

"What makes *you* think *you've* got what it takes?"

"There's a bunch of mashed potatoes eating the school…" Cathy murmured.

"Well, for starters, I don't fall over every time a shadow passes overhead."

"I don't strangle my teammates whenever there's a breeze."

"That was *one* time!"

"Okay then." Cathy's transformation caused a shockwave that blew Helen and Danni against the wall.

"Whoa!" Helen said as her back hit.

Cathy's hair was frizzy and hectic and her eyes bulged. She wore a tattered white uniform that appeared to have already taken battle damage. Torn strips of fabric hung from her arms as if she was a mental patient escaping the confines of a strait-jacket. She wore scruffy and dulled white pants to compliment, and a pair of beat-up sneakers with flying shoelaces that refused to remain tied. It was clear her struggle to think straight was affecting her ability to manifest a costume.

Helen picked at a dangling string, scrutinizing Cathy's weird wardrobe choice. "Are you wearing a straitjacket?"

"No." Cathy inspected her bizarre outfit and twitched once. "But it's comfy."

Their friend's manic behavior was becoming commonplace, so Danni and Helen shrugged to each other. They spread their arms and legs to make sure there was enough space between them and transformed together. The resulting shockwave finalized the destruction of a twenty-foot section of hallway outside the kitchen.

Cathy stared spacily at their damaged surroundings. "We have got to work on this..."

"Danni?"

"Yes, Helen?"

"Is that a yellow bodysuit?"

"I had to match *one* of you."

Danni wore a stylish cap-sleeved uniform with purple accents, a studded belt over a knee-length skirt, and shiny black boots so fancy they begged for a red carpet. Similar to Helen, but quite the opposite of Cathy's asylum-inspired apparel.

Helen studied her friends. They were ready and willing to stop Fruit Man from destroying the school, but neither of them expected to succeed. They put on poor masks of bravery to hide their fear and lack of confidence. Helen took Danni's hand in hers and placed the other on Cathy's shoulder. Danni did the same and they stood in a circle.

"Okay, we can do this." Helen swallowed hard. "We can."

"Lead on," Danni said. "For now."

Together, the three would-be heroes stepped into the doom-laden kitchen to face an undetermined fate.

Past the heated tubs and the stainless-steel counter, beyond the dusty milkshake machine and stacks of peanut butter and jelly sandwiches, a three-chamber sink overflowed with mashed potatoes, as if its faucet had tapped into an endless reservoir of the stuff. They poured out onto the floor and moved steadily through the kitchen, building up on themselves and spilling out into the hallway and beyond.

Three rigid and somewhat crystallized lunch ladies were stacked against the farthest wall, in various states of alarm. Off to the side, the peculiar lunch lady sat with her back to the flow. She observed her rescuers from a chair, where she was bound by the fast-hardening goop the girls were all too familiar with.

"It's Linda!" Helen exclaimed. "I thought you said she was fired!"

"Who are you?" the woman asked, dazed.

"We're here to help," said Danni.

"That's nice of you."

"First, where is he? Where's Fruit Man?" Helen scanned the kitchen, unconcerned with freeing the former lunch lady, at this time.

"I'm not sure."

Danni explained to Linda that they would be back for her and the girls continued. Fruit Man remained unseen, but no doubt, ready for them. They hadn't made it ten feet further into the kitchen before meeting his leading line of defense.

It was the smell that hit them first. A stench so putrid it invaded their nostrils, declaring war on each girl's olfactory nerve. It was the sickly-sweet smell of brown, rotting fruit—the decaying flesh of peaches, blackened banana peels, and withered melon rinds. There were sour grapes, dried halfway into raisins, and pungent pineapples, interspersed with hothouse tomatoes gone black. The myriad of odors created a rot so powerful the girls could taste it in their mouths. It hung so thick in the air that it stung their eyes and clung to their skin.

Helen, Cathy, and Danni gagged in unison, covering their mouths and noses, for what little good such actions could do.

"Ugh! What is that?" asked Danni.

Coughing, they searched for the source of the terrible smell and found it behind them, blue and green and fuzzy white. Helen recognized the vaguely humanoid form as what had become of the Fruit Man's Fruity Henchman.

His melon clogs were now cemented around his feet. Soft and browned, they were covered with tufts of white fuzz and they sloshed with soupy goo inside. His clothes, once adorned with colorful pieces of fruit and fruit peel, now hung in lumpy, blackened chunks. Fermenting syrup seeped down his body and pooled in the melons around his feet. His peach fuzz pants had grown positively hairy, and on his back, seedy strings of rotting tomato innards dripped like egg yolks from between the shriveled black cherry stems. On his head, the grapes were unrecognizable, forming a thick mat of bluish-grey mold, his hair replaced by thousands of floating black spores. What was once a normal student was now a giant's walking dose of penicillin.

Fruity Henchman shuffled closer, followed by a speckled halo of tiny flies. His movement was clumsy and slow, but the henchman no longer had to fight his victims to deter them. His aura of stench could envelop and overpower them without him lifting a finger.

"Somebody, do something," coughed Cathy.

"Danni," Helen ordered, "get tall and kick him again!"

"Nuh-uh!" Danni said. "Not with these boots! He's so gross. You do it—with your hair."

"I don't wanna touch him with my hair!" Helen cried. "You touch him!"

"You!"

"No, as leader, I order you!"

Cathy collapsed.

"Uh-oh," Danni and Helen said in unison.

"Can't breathe," choked Danni. "One of us has to do something."

Danni slumped to the floor, unconscious, and Helen dropped to her knees. Her hair fell limp around her. She squinted, her vision blurred, too dizzy to control her powers now. Through her creeping tunnel vision, she saw Fruit Man approach from behind the Fruity Henchman.

"Excellent, my henchman. Excellent. You have stopped them from *squashing* my plans."

Now on all fours, Helen resolved to herself never to hesitate again—If it wasn't already too late.

"Can I go home now?" asked Fruity Henchman.

"No," came the response. "You must guard the door to make sure others don't come to stop us."

"Oh, man…"

Helen gagged. Her vision was black, but she spoke to Fruit Man. "Just so you know…I think your henchman's…past his expiration date…"

With that, she too passed out.

CHAPTER TWENTY-EIGHT
"A certain stench"

Kat

When she saw the debris scattered across the floor, hanging wires, and cracks forming up the walls, Kat knew she had gone in the right direction. The floor was concave, like a small meteor had struck, leaving torn linoleum in its wake. She could no longer see the cafeteria through the surge of beige mashed potatoes. They blocked off the end of the hallway like a giant storm cloud.

In the damaged and flickering lights, Kat saw a dark blotch appear from the kitchen doorway, in front of the giant cloud. She was hit by a powerful odor, even from a fair distance away. The ends of her fingers tingled as her nails grew on impulse, black blades that retained the color of her polish.

The blotch marched toward her.

"Don't come any closer," it said. "Save yourself."

It was then Kat realized that the disgusting blotch was, in fact, the Fruity Henchman.

"What Fruit Man's doing is wrong," she said. "It's evil. And look what's happened to you. Why are you helping him?"

"Because," Fruity Henchman licked his chapped lips and squirmed a little as he tasted what was on them. "Because he's my friend. I won't let you pass."

Kat understood. She was beginning to learn what it meant to have true friends and now, she had to go help hers.

"I will get past you."

The Fruity Henchman reached into his cherry stem pack of goodies and scooped out two blackened lumps of something that once was fruity. He brought what was perhaps a watermelon rind up to his mouth, but he thought better of it, and whipped the rind at Kat as a makeshift boomerang instead.

With a flash of fingernail, the rind was halved, and the pieces flew by harmlessly. Fruity Henchman split his second lump in two, opaque brown juices squeezing between his dirty fingers. He threw the blobs at Kat, and they landed with repulsive splatters on the floor by her feet.

Kat gagged at the stench as it wafted up to her nostrils. What was once a tomato had become a very effective stink bomb.

Fruity Henchman took a difficult step forward. His speed had diminished as his suit decomposed around him. Kat heaved again as another wave of rot hit her. Frantically, she searched for a means to block the Fruity Henchman's most powerful weapon. Further along the ceiling, she found her stink shield. Kat took a deep, rancid breath and held it. Fruity Henchman took another step. And another. One more...

Kat sprinted forward. Still holding her breath, she rushed at the unprepared henchman. He put his arms up defensively and fell backward, expecting a violent collision. Kat jumped and used his shoulder to vault herself upward. With claws extended, she pierced her hand through the drop ceiling and jammed her fingers into whatever was above it. Kat hung there over the Fruity Henchman, surprised at her own ingenuity.

The need for fresh air compelled her to hurry as the henchman grappled at her legs. Kat kicked and flailed to keep him at bay. She slid an inch as her claws began to slice through the structure that was holding her up.

"Get away!" she said through gritted teeth, booting him down again.

Kat raised her free arm and aimed a finger at the sprinkler over her head. She had to get this just right. With one eye closed and body tense, she shot her claw forward, into the center of the mechanism. The pipe above them burst open and cold water showered over Kat and The Fruity Henchman. Kat fell back and hit the floor stumbling.

At first, the droplets spattered off of the thick layer of rot and decay that covered the henchman, but bit by bit, layers of filth sloughed from his head and torso. Clumps of who-knew-what fell to the floor with disgusting splat noises, into the thick puddle forming around Fruity Henchman's feet. Boy gradually separated from filth. His stench lessened enough that Kat could inhale without her lungs seizing.

Fruity Henchman was shivering, but his face was tilted up, into the raining droplets, eyes closed like he was enjoying the experience. Kat spotted a cloth undershirt peeking through the grime and she sprang to grab the boy by the collar, shaking him out of his trance.

"Now whatcha gonna do?" she menaced.

Fruity Henchman blinked. "He told me to stop you."

"He's the one who needs stopped, and you know it." Kat thought she saw tears mingling with the filthy water that ran down the boy's cheeks. "Go home," she said. "Take a shower. Let us handle it from here."

The boy slumped to the floor and Kat let go of his shirt. She made for the kitchen doorway. Her friends were in there, but there was no commotion, no fighting—a bad sign.

Danni

Cold water pooled around her face. Danni's eyes fluttered open. There was a horrible taste in her mouth—remnants of the powerful odor that had affected her. Cathy groaned next to her. Something was moving on top of her legs. It was Helen.

Footsteps splashed on the tile floor and an intimidating pair of black combat boots stopped in front of Danni's nose. A hand surrounded by fingerless fishnet gloves reached into her vision. Danni followed the netting up its arm, to Kat Crenshaw's icy blue stare. She was transformed, all in black.

Kat raised an arched brow: *Well?*

Danni took the offered hand, and Kat helped her up from the floor. As she stood, it dawned on Danni that the hallway's sprinkler head had been triggered.

She gasped. "Oh my gosh! Is there a fire?"

"No," Kat said. "I had to wash off a certain stench."

Danni asked, "What made you come back?"

"Let's just say Priscilla isn't the only stuck-up snob in this school. And I'm not about to make that mistake again."

"That makes no sense to me," Helen said, "but it's good to have you back."

There was a loud crash behind them. The mashed potatoes surged with enough power to break through part of the wall, splintering the door jamb as they grew to even greater proportions. They spilled further into the kitchen and the girls backpedaled to avoid getting swallowed.

"Woah! What's going on now?" Danni asked.

"No potatoes. No please. Don't eat me please." Linda's chair had been toppled by the surge and she lay on her side while the potatoes absorbed her lower body. "Nice potatoes, good potatoes—You lie!—I mean, *lovely* potatoes…"

"Quick!" Helen shouted, "Get her outta that stuff!"

Danni and Cathy hurried to grab the chair. Danni grew in size and tugged, but the potatoes continued to consume Linda.

"They're not letting go!" Danni cried.

"Don't worry, Linda!" Helen rushed over. "We'll have to dig her out. Keep pulling!"

Kat

Kat watched with disgust as Helen cupped her hands and dug into the food product around the woman's waist. She would need help. The tingling sensation from Kat's fingertips traveled up her wrists. Her nails expanded, connected, and covered her forearms, creating curved black spades. She ran to Linda's other side and hastily cut into the potatoes as well. When Helen noticed what Kat had accomplished with her powers, she grinned.

Kat scowled. "What?"

"You-oove be-en practicinnnng," Helen sang.

Kat tossed a scoop of potatoes at Helen's obnoxious face, and Linda was freed. With the side of her arm, Kat cracked open Linda's restraints and the lady clambered to her feet and brushed herself off.

"Oh that was quite marvelous!" Linda spewed, taking in the various talents of the girls around her. She grabbed Danni's hand at chest height. "You're so tall—and you're so pointy!"

"Okay…" Kat accepted Linda's enthusiastic handshake.

"And your hair—so beautifully long!"

As Linda wobbled her arm next, Helen asked, "How is Fruit Man controlling the potatoes? We have to get to him—before the kitchen is gone!"

"They lie!" Linda cried. "They make you think they can be controlled but they cannot!"

"How do we stop them?" Kat said.

"Dehydrated Mashed Generic Potatoes: Made in Taiwan," Linda recited, "Add one half teaspoon to ten gallons of water. Mix in large dough mixer ten minutes, fourteen point seven seconds. Will produce twenty gallons."

Kat stared. Linda's cryptic explanation did nothing. She really was as strange as they had said.

"Ooh! Ooh!" Cathy hopped up and down, raising her arm. Once she had everyone's attention, she spurted, "No water!"

"Oh, great!" Danni said, tapping her foot in the growing puddle that had flooded the kitchen.

Kat threw her hands in the air. "How was I supposed to know?"

"He put the whole box in the wash sink and left the faucet running," Linda said.

A voice hissed from behind them. "And there's no way to stop it now!"

CHAPTER TWENTY-NINE
"The Space Takers"

Helen

"**F**ruit Man!" Helen called, in true comic book fashion. She and her teammates whipped around to face their enemy.

"The potatoes have multiplied beyond anyone's control!" he exclaimed. "Soon, the school will be destroyed, engulfed by the very thing that was to be the pinnacle of its budgetary salvation!"

"But why?" asked Danni. "What do you have to gain from destroying the school?"

"Revenge!" came the response. He pointed to the sugarfied lunch ladies against the wall. "They did this to us, and for what? For money? For test scores? It was the ingestion of these potatoes that made me the wretched being you now see before you

—a creature who suffers with insatiable hunger! They must pay for the wrongdoings that have been wrought upon my person. The obliteration of Pearson Middle School is the logical next phase of my inglorious transformation. First Pearson Middle School, then New Potentia, then the country! Then—"

"The world? Yeah, we get it," Helen said. "That was some speech. Did you spend all night writing it with a thesaurus?"

"As a matter of fact, I did!" Fruit Man created a crystal boulder and threw it in their direction.

Everyone jumped away.

"So, you're going to destroy the world, too?" Danni asked in disbelief.

"Aiming a little high, aren't we?" Helen scoffed, "A little tall?"

Fruit Man broke out of his reverie, incensed by Helen's biting comment. "And who are you to stop me?"

"We're the Space Takers!" Kat shouted.

With a surge of pride, Helen, Cathy, and Danni looked at one another. They each began to smile and they repeated, in unison, "The Space Takers!"

"You are fools!" Fruit Man said.

He extended his arms and tentacles of slithering goo materialized from his palms, barreling toward the four with blinding speed. Helen dashed in front of her friends and created a shield of hair which fanned out behind her like a mushroom cap, enclosing even Linda behind a fibrous red wall. She stiffened her tresses to defend against the sugary onslaught, and she shuddered as the gunk sank in.

"Guh…"

The others gawked at her.

"Never hesitate," she ordered.

"What's that on your chest?" Danni asked, pointing.

"It's on all our suits," said Kat. "See? Mine's pink."

Cathy exclaimed, "It's my symbol! The one I've been drawing everywhere!"

"But what does it mean?" Helen asked.

"Well, it's not pie," Danni said.

"Don't you see?" Kat explained. "It's us. It's the symbol of a person with her arms and legs spread out. The way we stand to transform."

"Huh." Helen remarked. It was time to make a plan. "Now, that we've finally become a team," she said, "the first thing we have to do is split up. Danni, you and Kat stop the mashed potatoes—find a way to shut off the water. Cathy and I will stop Fruit Man, or at least buy enough time for you to get back and help us."

She pointed at Linda. "While we've got him distracted, you drag those other lunch ladies out of the way. Get them out of here if you can wake them up."

Linda nodded, her eyes as bug-like as ever, and her untamed hair shaking atop her scalp. Cathy stood next to her, with her own wild hair and equally wide glasses.

"Did you eat the potatoes, too?" she asked.

"Everyone ready?" Helen said. "Go!"

With a flourish, Helen tossed aside her heavily sugared tresses. Cathy charged with pent-up energy raging. She collided with Fruit Man and sent him tumbling backwards into the wall. Linda ran in one direction, Kat and Danni in the other, leaving Helen to squirm and hop around with disgust.

"Cripes! It's in my hair! It's in my hair!"

Cathy returned to where Helen was whining and said, "Bugs on a windshield."

"What?"

"Rotten fruit suit."

"Cathy, what?"

Cathy shook her head to clear it. "Could be worse!" She explained.

"Right." Helen stopped her balking. "Stay with me, okay?"

Cathy nodded.

Fruit Man resumed his assault by forming a sugar crystal in his fist. He threw it as a projectile that struck Cathy in the side of her head, toppling her and cracking her glasses. Incensed by Cathy's painful fall, Helen ran at Fruit Man, and they locked hands, each straining against the other's strength. Sandy, gooey sugar squished between their fingers.

The villain's milky white stare glowed in malevolence. Clear syrup seeped from his eyes, drizzling down his glazed and powdery face. Inches away, Helen could see that deep within those eyes, two dark pupils struggled to peer through the visions of malice clouding them.

Helen took a hard-fought step forward, pushing Fruit Man back on the sopping wet floor.

He howled. "I won't lose to a girl!"

An unnerving cold radiated from Helen's palms, followed by a weakness in her arms and a glowing light around their inter-locked hands. Helen panted as powerlessness tugged at her core. Fruit Man was draining her energy, converting her into yet another depleted victim. She should have known not to touch him! Helen released her grip, but her foe clenched his fingers tighter. As the cold followed her arms into her chest, Helen's hair flew in to save her. It wedged itself between Helen and Fruit Man. Strands of it squeezed between their palms and methodically pried them apart.

Helen fell away, crawling backwards and scrambling to her feet. She clutched her chest, brandishing her hair around herself as Cathy came to her side. A big, comical lump had emerged on Cathy's temple, purple with bruising.

"Lose to a girl," she insisted, parrot-like.

This enraged Fruit Man further. Goo pooled out from under his feet and shot across the floor. It gathered around their ankles and climbed their legs. Cathy and Helen fell back against each other as it solidified around their torsos.

"Ugh. This stuff is starting to get on my nerves." Helen said as she strained.

Fruit Man sauntered up to them, triumphant. "Now I have a question for you…"

They awaited the interrogation with defiant expressions.

"What kind of fruit will never run away and get married?"

Helen tilted her head, perplexed at this line of questioning.

"You!" cried Fruit Man. "For you shall never escape this kitchen alive!"

"Cantaloupe?" Cathy asked.

"Can't elope." Helen agreed.

Cathy proceeded to shake herself and Helen free from the block of sugar that held them.

CHAPTER THIRTY
"I think we got the hard job"

Danni

With Cathy's speedy distraction, Danni and Kat sprinted back through the kitchen and up, over the sneeze guards, to dive below the lunch line and out of sight. Crouched below the tray shelf, the two paused to catch their breath.

"Sure would be a terrible time for asthma," Danni said, glad that their shared conditions never manifested during their transformations.

"How the heck are we supposed to shut off the water?" Kat shook her head. "Fruit Man's right—there's no way to reach the sink now."

"That wouldn't be enough anyway, with the sprinklers."

"I get it! I'm sorry already."

"I'm sure it was a good idea at the time," Danni said. "You know, I think we got the hard job."

"There's gotta be a source somewhere in this school to control all the water," Kat said.

Danni put a hand on Kat's shoulder. "Did you hear that?"

Kat stared at Danni's hand, uncomfortable. "Hear what?"

A muffled voiced cried out from within the rolling mounds of mashed potato.

"Come on." Danni dashed out through the remaining doorway and back toward the wall of spuddy doom that blocked the cafeteria. "I heard a moan, like someone's in there."

Under the rushing sprinkler once again, Kat yelled, "Then they're a gonner!"

The noise sounded again, this time louder and closer. It was stifled, yet there could be no mistake:

MOOOOOO!

"I'm going in," said Danni. "Hold my legs."

"Seriously?"

Danni dove, head first, into the squishy mass. Her feet remained on the floor, but her legs stretched forth, following her body into the mashed potatoes. She heard Kat's voice:

"Are you crazy?"

The potatoes began to swell, and Kat took hold of Danni's ankles to pull her back against the suction.

Danni fought the urge to sneeze as the spuds squished up her nostrils. At first, the overgrown side dish was clammy and cold around her body. But as she stretched deeper into the core, she was overcome by a warmth that both disturbed and compelled her. She was surrounded by cushions, pampered by the enveloping softness.

A tug at her legs, and Danni broke out of her trance. She resisted the potatoes' enchantment and waved her arms to beat off the sensation around her. Her weakness gone, she pushed on, swimming through the mash. With her eyes shut tight, Danni reached out for another person's arm or leg. She stretched more and reached out again, until her air ran out and she had to return to the hallway.

Danni concentrated on restoring her proportional form and she shrank backwards, her bones shortening and her skin reducing. When her fingers brushed against something solid, Danni reacted and grabbed it.

Kat

Kat shuddered as Danni's bony ankles changed beneath her palms. It was an unsettling experience, even through the boots, which shifted and conformed to Danni's body. When Danni emerged, she had her hands clasped around a familiar blue and white object. The object belted out another loud *moo* as it hit the air, a second pair of hands clutching to it. Kat and Danni managed to pull free Principal Pal, who had a death grip on his sabotaged megaphone.

The school principal had had his precious machine cupped around his face to maintain an air pocket after being swallowed by the tidal wave. With his mouth gaping open and shut, he gulped in oxygen like a fish on dry land.

Danni stooped next to him, hands on her knees, covered in side dish. She resembled a small yeti, but patches of her yellow bodysuit had managed to stay visible from beneath the white fluff of mashed potatoes. To be precise, she resembled a small yeti—that had peed itself—and was wearing fashionable black boots.

"Ask him," she told Kat as she scraped herself off. "He'd know where we could get to the main source."

"It wasn't supposed to be like this," Principal Pal sobbed. "…He said they—the test scores—some kind of a mistake…"

"Um, what's he talking about?" Danni asked.

"Who cares?" Kat had no patience for the shady man and his whining. She grabbed him by his lapels and shook him. "Where do we go to turn off the water?"

Linda

"Oh, oh B—B—" *Bearded-one* was what Linda wanted to say, but it was not the lady's name. "B—B—"

Linda wiped clean the little powdered rectangle pinned to the woman's apron, and revealed the bearded one's true name: "Maude."

"Get up B—Maude," Linda goaded.

The lunch lady groaned, but did not budge. Linda moved over to the wart-nosed one, who wore a nametag that read "Beatrice." She, too, was unresponsive. The ladies' rigid faces seemed all the more absurd under layers of caked-on makeup. Drained, colorless cheeks beneath circles of bright blush. Linda next shook the third fallen lunch lady—"Susan"—the too-much-lipsticked one, who resembled Pagliacci the clown, mid aria.

"Please awaken!"

One of the girls who had helped save Linda sprinted behind her, cartwheeling to dodge pale streams of syrup. Goo splatted against the wall where Linda knelt. She yelped and dashed to the walk-in refrigerator, swung open the door, and ducked inside, out of harm's way.

The door shut behind her and the chaotic noise outside was instantly subdued. Linda hid in a dark cocoon, panting tiny clouds into the cold. She shuddered. Not from the temperature, but from the idea that the school's misdeeds had come back to destroy it.

"It's finally happened!" Linda caught her mouth in her hands.

She had been telling them all along how wrong they were to shirk nutrition in favor of cheap, easy-to-prepare foodstuffs. But they wouldn't listen to her warnings. They wouldn't listen to her alternatives. Part of her wished for this Fruit Man to succeed in destroying what had created him. They had allowed him to carry on, in order to save face and now they would reap the consequences. Part of her desired revenge, too—for having her job taken from her so she could no longer watch over the children of the lunch line.

Thoughts like this leaked in from time to time, but Linda never obeyed that part of her. It was the angry part of her that made her like everyone else. It was not the part of her that talked to the fruits and vegetables. It was not the part that heard the whispers in the refrigerator around her.

CHAPTER THIRTY-ONE
"I might actually be going insane"

Helen

By now, the floors of the kitchen had been covered in a thick mixture of potato, water, and sugar-slime that made it difficult for Helen to find footing. Disgusting puddles pooled on the surface, soaking into her shoes.

Cathy's legs still moved at blinding speed, but the floor was too slippery to gain decent traction. Slimy spuds sputtered up from her fast-moving feet. This made her little more than a moving target for Fruit Man to shoot at, rather than a speeding bullet for him to dodge.

Helen's hair was sopping wet, doubling its weight and making it a sluggish weapon. The upside was that it slid through the majority of Fruit Man's snares like buttered string through the eye of a greased needle. But it swung clumsily, too tangled to manifest itself in the form of tentacle-appendages anymore.

Fruit Man battered at them with giant rocks for fists. When swinging the heavy weights around on the ends of his arms tired him, he would suck the sugar back into his system to shoot some more. Helen had hoped she and Cathy could cause him to deplete his power, but it was becoming obvious now that this was not going to happen. Fruit Man was reabsorbing everything he was using up. A luminous aura had formed in the air from the sludge around him.

Helen was painfully aware that, in this small space, there was nowhere she or Cathy could retreat to in order to avoid getting drained themselves, should Fruit Man determine he was weakening.

If only there was a way to drain it all at once, she thought, *or to knock him out completely with one powerful attack*.

The opponents faced off against each other in a triangle. Fruit Man opened and closed his fists, bursting with energy as goop oozed between his fingers. He had the sneering visage of a lunatic, clear syrup dripping from his eyes and mouth.

Helen's fists were clenched, as if she could fight her rival hand to hand. Her hair flared out, a giant flowing cape which undulated behind her, prepared to lunge at its enemy.

Cathy jittered.

The opponents were tensed, preparing to attack once again, when the refrigerator door burst open. Linda leapt from the walk-in, trailing a crowd of very unexpected—very animate—produce. This astonishing advance caught everyone off guard, but with the lunch lady at the head of the assault, Helen was relieved. The cavalry was here!

"Yeah!" Helen exclaimed.

"I think it's time somebody got me a real straightjacket," Cathy said, starrily. "I might actually be going in-sane..."

Fruit Man's concentration faded, replaced by a glimmer of fear.

"Quickly!" Linda shouted to her harvested minions. "To the blenders!"

Linda darted past the three students who were entwined in deadly battle. Her fruity followers hopped, bopped, and wobbled through the muck. Helen, Cathy, and Fruit Man stared, following the impossible parade to its destination, a row of industrial blenders, dusty from neglect.

"Carrots!" Linda yelled. Bundles of carrots sprung forth to pry the lids off of the blenders. "Strawberry, apple, banana!"

Linda orchestrated, a deranged maestro, pointing into which blender each piece of fruit should hop. And, like lemmings, the devoted fruit obeyed, nestling themselves against the blades of the machines.

"Zucchini!" she ordered. "And—yessss—beets!"

As the symphony continued, Linda summoned three giant watermelons from the back shelves of the refrigerator. They bounded forth with as much gruesome determination as their brethren, splattering themselves against the back wall to spill their juices into the blenders below and drown the mish mash huddled within. But Linda was not yet finished.

"Honey!" she called. "Yogurt!" she added. "Cinnamon, turmeric, spinach, kale!"

Inanimate items were brought to her on rafts of rolling carrot logs before Linda added them to their peculiar concocttions. The ingredients Linda ordered grew more specific, until Linda was shouting, "Where are my omega-3's?"

Helen was barely aware that her mouth was agape this whole time.

The carrots were the last to jump into the blenders.

Linda's face was one of crazed anticipation as she said, "Puree!"

The scene that ensued was horrific. There was no mercy for the minions. Splotches of fruit and veggie viscera splattered against the glass inside the machines before oozing back down to the blades to splatter up again.

Humming to herself, Linda reached below the countertop— below the whirling blenders—to retrieve three paper cups. A trio of juicy grapes bounced their way across the metal to the nearest storage shelf. Each impaled itself upon a straw and rolled its catch back to Linda.

Helen swallowed hard. The cavalry had been slaughtered.

Linda's horde was clearly harmless to anything but itself, so Fruit Man resumed his attack on Helen and Cathy.

"Okay," Helen said, dodging, "she's got an army of fruit. Why are *you* called Fruit Man, again?"

Danni

Droplets of water trickled from the rushing pipes above them. The eerie *spats* they made against the floor were the only noises to accompany the girls' echoing footfall. The darkened passageway was dirty, dank, and dingy. A number of less-than-preferable d-words came to Danni's mind as she traversed the basement hallway with Kat, heading toward the bowels of the school.

Heaped and forgotten trash carts waited, leftover from Murphy's convalescence. They lined the far wall, leaking weeks' old cafeteria waste down the corridor. The brick walls were slimy and mildewed, and broken tiles cracked beneath their feet. Bones of many a rodent-like creature were scattered along the sides of the hall.

The d-word that came to mind most vividly was "dungeon."

A flickering florescent bulb hummed over their path, just bright enough to keep the two of them from tripping on the uneven ground as they followed the stinking trash ooze to its destination.

"I don't think this basement's up to code," Kat murmured, her eyes darting from one hazard to the next.

Danni gulped. "Principal Pal is still trying to cover up the potatoes. He sent us down here, knowing we wouldn't come back again."

"Danni, there's no way to hide the potatoes now. Don't worry. All this is, is a long, creepy hallway with a bunch of pipes at the end of it."

"Just the same," Danni whispered, "in scary situations such as these, there is nothing to be ashamed of about holding hands for comfort."

Kat stopped in her tracks and scowled up at Danni.

"Or not. Just a suggestion."

Kat moved on, with Danni trailing close behind. A dim light shone from an unknown source in front of them, illuminating their faces as they approached. Danni peered out from behind her shoulders. They had reached the mouth of a large room, scarcely brightened by one dusty round lamp, nestled at the peak of the tall, domed ceiling above them. The room was cast in a sinister crimson hue that leaked out from around the hatch of the school's roaring incinerator.

The water pump rested in its shadow, along the curved wall. Rusted and leaky pipes snaked around, climbing up the bricks like living vines and forming a labyrinth of intertwined metal.

Scattered throughout the room, old and decrepit pieces of furniture had splintered apart with time. There were tables, a couple of dilapidated chairs, and the remnants of ancient filing cabinets, with drawers no longer attached to their hinges.

Bits of wood and broken-down metal mingled with everything from office stationery to landscaping sod in a large pile of junk that was shoveled off to the side, all waiting to burn. The congealing ooze of the neglected trash wound its way through the pile to a circular drain in the middle of the floor. Otherwise, the room was empty.

"See?" Kat said. "All we have to do is find a valve or something. Nothing to be scared of."

As they crossed the middle of the room, a long, slow creak stopped them in their tracks. Kat and Danni slid back-to-back and spun around.

Their frightened eyes settled on the pile of junk. As the noise continued, the pile heaped itself upward. Pieces of debris shifted from place to place, settling into a humanoid form, which rose above the girls. A dented globe rolled up to the top of the form, followed by a familiar cracked magnifying glass. Kat recognized the items. From somewhere within the mass, a lamp clicked on, and Mrs. Francis's broken overhead projector shined its light through the magnifying lens, encasing Danni and Kat in its gaze.

A crescendo of noises blew forth from the creature and the girls ducked and covered their ears. Forgotten coins jingled. Rusty hinges screeched. Broken wooden boards splintered apart and banged together. Unknown items rubbed against each other, rusty wheels squeaked, and papers tore themselves apart. It was as if the creature was taking stock of every possible sound it could make. Ultimately, it chose a single noise to use, expressing its intent. If the globe and magnifying glass were to be this creature's mismatched eyes, then the trombone slide that came rolling out from the mass beneath took on the role of a makeshift tongue.

It towered over Kat and Danni who were holding hands with white-knuckled grips.

CHAPTER THIRTY-TWO
"Giant-scary-monster things"

Danni

Danni's body trembled, caught inside the creature's looming shadow. She and Kat stood terrified, trapped and blinded by its projector-spotlight.

The creature's trombone blared menacingly: "WHA WHA WA HA WHA WHA?"

There was a pause. Was the creature waiting for a response?

"WHA WHA WA HA WHA WHA?" it demanded again.

"Answer it!" Kat prodded Danni in the side with her elbow.

"What? How?"

"You're in band," Kat explained in an incensed whisper. "You can musicspeak."

"That's the dumbest thing—"

"*WHA WHA WA HA WHA WHA!*" the creature proclaimed.

"Oh…" Danni cocked her head, perplexed. A basic intention flowed through the creature's notes. "It said something like, 'Who goes there?'"

"So, answer it!" Kat pushed her up toward the creature.

The creature stomped forward, one leg an overturned classroom desk. The other, a wobbly swivel chair which was missing a wheel. Its body shook viciously, with nothing concrete to hold it together and a shower of misshapen paper clips scattered across the floor. Another stomp, and it rained push pins.

"Uh, we're the S-space Tay…" she faltered.

Danni felt a buzzing in her brain. The next instant, she was flat on the floor, a rake swishing overhead. Danni rolled onto her back, beneath her attacker. From this vantage point, she could see straight up into the creature. What she saw frightened her more than anything she had experienced so far. There was nothing to it but parts—no man in a junk-gathering costume, no super robot magnet to hold the pieces together—just free-flowing, self-sticking fragments which worked in unison.

As impossible as it seemed for such a creature to exist, seeing it didn't surprise her. With rampaging mashed potatoes currently devouring the school, all bets were off. Danni could have taken a moment to ponder how such a thing came to exist, but instead, she rolled out of the way to dodge a cascade of inkless pens and broken pencils. The creature was taking another step toward Kat.

"Danni!" Kat called.

"I'm alright," she coughed.

"BREWWEEERWU WAH WAH HONK!"

The creature lunged, its spotlight now focused on Kat. With an "Eep," Kat jumped back to avoid its sweeping arms. The creature gave chase, its clumsy footfall echoing bangs and squeaks around the room as it followed her. Danni got to her feet, hoping to help her teammate.

Her abrupt movement caught the creature's attention and it swiveled on its clunky chair leg to change course. For the next minutes, the three played a disturbing game of tag, in which to be caught had unknown, but terrifying consequences. Danni and Kat caught up with each other and ran circles around the room.

"What on earth is that?" Danni yelled. "Why is it here?"

"Because *of course* it is!" Kat yelled back, her voice cracking. "Of course, there's something here to make this ten times harder than it has to be!"

When the scent hit her nose, Danni asked, "What about those trash bags? What's leaking out of them?"

"Who cares?"

"Maybe something from the trash is causing—"

"The nerds are upstairs, Danni! It doesn't matter why it's here!"

"But what does it want?" Danni hollered above the noise of the incinerator as they passed.

"It's a giant scary monster!" Kat said. "It wants to do giant-scary-monster things!"

Danni scoffed. "You're so closedminded."

"The thing's got a rake for a hand!" Kat shrieked.

"HONK BEEP HINK FWA WAH HA WAH!"

"It's trying to tell us something," Danni said.

"Never mind what it's saying! When I count to three, let's make a break for the hallway."

"Wait!" Danni took Kat by the arm to halt her. "We still have to stop the water."

Kat wrenched her arm away from her teammate. "We still have to keep breathing."

"Shh!" Danni put her finger to her lips.

The creature had gone silent. The creaks and scrapes had ceased. It was lumped on the floor, as inconspicuous as it had been when they entered. Now, it wheezed quietly, heaving up and down as if it was sobbing.

Sympathetic Danni, full of compassion, approached the creature. "What's wrong with it?"

"It's a trap," Kat responded, reaching for her teammate.

"Maybe it's hurt or something."

"Are you crazy?"

Danni continued to draw near the heaving pile with the tender concern of a big sister. "Um, excuse me? Are you okay?"

The creature shifted, startling Danni. It studied her with its shining magnifying glass and gently swiveling globe.

"FWA?" blew the timid horn.

"Is that it?" asked Danni.

"What's it saying?"

"Is that what you want?"

"Danni! What's it saying? Does it want our souls?"

"FWA?" the creature repeated.

"'Cause we should definitely get out of here if it wants our souls!"

"It wants to be our friend."

"*Friend?*"

Before she could think better of it, Danni's outgoing personality prompted her to answer, "Of course we'll be your friends!"

The junk creature rose up and bellowed with every sound in its body. The tongue-horn blared. "FWAAAAA!"

"Bad idea!" Kat said. "Bad idea!"

Danni tiptoed backward as the creature continued to thrash about excitedly. It creaked towards them, its makeshift arms extended to embrace its newfound companions.

"Uh, the hallway?" Kat suggested.

"Yeah," whispered Danni.

The two dashed to escape this fresh predicament, but the creature anticipated and leapt to block the exit. Pieces of broken wood splintered out as it impacted with the floor, and its two would-be friends grabbed each other and screamed in terror.

"FFWWWAAAAAAA!"

"AAAAAAAHHHHHHHH!"

Screaming "Fwa," it charged at them once again. Kat and Danni separated and fled in opposite directions. With amazing dexterity, the creature swiveled on its wobbly chair leg and turned its pursuit in Kat's direction. It had gained fresh intensity, uplifted at the prospect of its brand-new friend-ships. It caught up to Kat before she could even round the room.

Kat must have felt the creature's fast approach behind her. She spun to face her attacking devotee and Danni watched helplessly as it scooped Kat up into the air. Her nails couldn't grow fast enough to aid her escape, but she used them frantically on the various pieces of junk that made up the creature's arm. Rolled up in a fist of sod and scraggly chicken wire, Kat swiped at everything in front of her. Despite destroying numerous items, she made little progress. Each damaged thing was replaced by another from the bulk of the creature's body.

"Danniiii…" she called.

Danni was too busy saving her own self to help her ensnared friend. Even as it snatched Kat off the floor, the creature had shifted direction again and gone after its other new *fwa*. As Danni fled to escape, the meter in her head shifted and sent her rolling to the floor. The rake passed over her as she somersaulted forward and jumped back to her feet. The creature retracted its weapon, and replaced the landscaping tool with a tattered fire hose. Danni yelped and did her best to run faster, elongating her legs to create a bigger stride. The hose whipped at her and, with another *click*, Danni dove to the side, safe again. As she scrambled away, crawling underneath one of the dilapidated tables, Danni was racking her brain.

How many was that? How many more ducks do I have left?

Kat

Kat was more frightened now than she had been when she thought the creature wanted to kill her. She wriggled some more, trying to free herself from the its grasp. For a pile of discarded junk, it was incredibly strong.

From her new vantage point, eight feet up in the air, Kat searched the creature for any sign of weakness she could exploit. Something had to be controlling it from somewhere. It had to have a brain or a heart—*something*. As it fumbled for Danni, it flipped a table across the room and Kat caught sight of one immobile object in the center of the form. She squinted past the many moving pieces of scrap to see a small, vague figure, mimicking the shape of the creature. One stubby arm was held in, as if keeping Kat at its side. The other reached outward, causing the hose to extend toward Danni. Kat dug her hands into the creature and shot her claws through the figure within, ripping it from the chest.

The creature went still.

Then it collapsed where it stood, scattering its various parts across the entire room. Kat dropped from her airborne position and she managed to land triumphantly on her feet. The hose fell limp to the floor at Danni's side, and she looked up from where she had been cowering against the wall.

"…You broke it?"

Kat showed Danni the object as she removed it from her claws. It was a ragged, worn, and stringy stuffed animal. Danni approached with a compassionate whimper.

"Aw, someone's abandoned little teddy bear. No wonder he wanted a friend."

"Yeah," Kat reached for the heavy incinerator door and swung it open with a grunt.

"What are you doing?" Danni said.

"We have to destroy this."

Danni jumped in between Kat and the raging fire. "No! You can't!"

"Fire destroys everything."

"It's too sad."

"Fine," Kat said. "You figure out what to do with it."

She tossed the tattered bear to her teammate, who gasped and reached out to catch it.

Click.

Danni's arms swished past the bear and folded over her face as she crumpled to the ground instead. The bear disappeared into the inferno and Kat stepped over Danni to close the door.

Danni's jaw dropped. "You did that on purpose!"

Kat swallowed hard. "We've got a job to do." She pointed. "There's the valve. Do you think you can reach it?"

CHAPTER THIRTY-THREE

"New plan"

Linda

Linda poured each smoothie into the mouth of a lunch lady. Their frozen screams of terror made this a simple task. Each of her cocktails was specifically concocted for one of them. One may have needed the potassium found in a button mushroom's stem, while the other required the blend of vitamins found in the skin of the Fuji apple.

Linda's recipes were so detailed and precise that each of the fallen lunch ladies immediately responded. Color returned to their cheeks and their rigid fingers twitched. Within moments, the three were sitting up and sucking on the grape-adorned straws of their various drinks.

"What happened?" asked Beatrice.

"The last thing I saw was Linda. She attacked us!" spat Susan, a raspberry-colored syrup dribbling down her chin.

"No, it was someone else," said Maude. "I saw him—a student."

"It was the Fruit Man," Linda explained.

"FM?" Susan asked. "I thought you were FM."

"No, but I created him." Linda's voice was cold. "We all did."

The lunch ladies reflected on her words as they sipped at their drinks.

Maude was the first to notice their surroundings, "What on earth are we sitting in?"

Beatrice squirmed. "Is this mashed potatoes?"

"What's going on here?" Susan demanded.

"The Fruit Man put the box of dehydrated generic mashed potatoes: made in Taiwan in the sink."

"Holy majolie! It'll destroy the school!" Maude shouted.

"We have to get out of here!" Susan climbed to her feet with surprising geriatric speed, as did her fellow lunch ladies.

Feeling much better now, the three made a break for the kitchen's back door. With a snap of Linda's fingers, two giant stalks of sugar cane zipped out of nowhere and barred the door with a large X. Susan pulled on the handle, but the sugar cane held fast. She and the other lunch ladies twisted around, equally fearful and confused about Linda's uncanny new power over food items.

"Since when do we have sugar cane?" asked Beatrice.

"Let us go," Susan pleaded. "We need to escape."

"We need to help the Space Takers," Linda insisted.

"The what?"

"We need cornstarch."

Helen

Helen and Cathy had made no headway in wearing down Fruit Man. It was time to try something new. Helen's hair had grown sluggish, weighed down by the muck that filled the kitchen. She told Cathy to keep him busy while she recovered.

For her part, Cathy zipped from shelf to shelf—bits of food, plastic silverware, boxes of foil and cling wrap—whatever could be found stored throughout the kitchen, she slung it at their enemy, all the while never giving Fruit Man the chance to zero in on her location and retaliate.

The items were aimed accurately, but none reached their target. With the incredible reflexes of someone who played too many video games, he was able to anticipate each projectile, and stop it in midair with a well-placed goop strike. Each can, colander, and can opener landed with a disheartening splat in the muck.

The next thing Cathy grabbed was a long bag of stacked paper cups. She whirled it around with a loud "Hwaaaaa" and struck a pose in front of her enemy. She lifted a brow to give him the bulging stink eye. Cathy's makeshift nunchucks and ultra-intimidating gaze did little to scare the Fruit Man, but it was only meant to be a distraction.

Helen had finished wringing out her hair, making it light enough to swing around again. Her intent was to wrap it around Fruit Man and entwine him so he could not escape. It was a risky plan—she had no idea whether or not he could drain her energy through her hair or from whatever distance she was able to keep him.

As Helen swung the cumbersome mass that had once been her beautifully flowing tresses, Fruit Man slipped by, skating through his own sugary slime. He received a stack of cups to the cranium for his evasion, but they did little to hinder his escape. Helen's hair was still too heavy to be effective, but she used the same desperate maneuver that had gotten her in trouble so many times before. With a heave, she whipped the weighty mass over her head, attempting to bring it down, and topple the fleeing Fruit Man.

Fruit Man countered with the obvious defense and pinned Helen's hair to the ceiling with crystalized goo. He threw his head back to laugh, but this time, Helen was prepared for her predicament. She wrapped her fists around the body of her hair and swung herself across the kitchen, kicking Fruit Man with outstretched legs. Waves of watery potato splashed around his sailing body, and he slid into the far wall, leaving the tile floor visible in his wake.

While the boy recovered from his bewilderment, Helen called her teammate over. She tugged at her hair, loosening it from the ceiling's infernal grip as Cathy skidded to a halt.

"Cathy, you're gonna have to get out of here, next time there's a chance. I don't know what happened to Danni and Kat, but those potatoes have to be stopped *now*. You have to go find them, find the water source."

The water in the hallway stopped.

"Oh, it's about time!" Helen yelled up at the nearest sprinkler. She turned to her teammate. "New plan, Cathy. You keep distracting him with your speed 'n' stuff. I'll see if I can't get another shot in. Maybe I can knock him into the potatoes while they've still got some life left in 'em."

"M-But…"

A surge of sludge rose from beneath Helen and scooped her up. Fruit Man had come to his senses, and from his hands and knees, he controlled the sugar-slime mixture that had been accumulating within the potatoes on the floor around them. A huge slimy fist lifted Helen from the floor and slammed her back into the sludge. The mixture was so deep she had to fight to keep her nose and mouth in the air above it while the clammy goop seeped into her ear canals. She caught her breath as a shell began to creep around the edges of her face.

Fruit Man chuckled fiendishly. "I'm feeling a little hungry. I think I'll cocoon you like a spider does a fruit fly."

"Cathy!" Helen cried.

Cathy

What a time for Cathy's wits to fail her! Waves of slick sugar pressed over Helen, even as she thrashed against them, sloshing around in a lake of potatoes. Her sweet coating had blocked her ears and covered her forehead. It was climbing across her chin.

Cathy could see her friend was in trouble. She had to do something, but she couldn't get past the thought of how horrible Helen's motley mixture would taste. Cathy couldn't move. Had Fruit Man entrapped her too? No, but her feet were planted in the potatoes, refusing to uproot themselves, no matter how politely she asked them.

"Speed 'n' stuff!" Cathy grabbed her head. *Focus!* Helen had given her so many orders she couldn't decide which one to follow. She concentrated on her last command. "Speed 'n' stuff!"

Helen tried to shout new orders, but her words muffled as the shell slipped over her mouth.

Here, Cathy's best friend needed her—a literal matter of life and death. Cathy jittered. She hopped. The stress of the situation was too much for her fragile transformed psyche to handle. Inside, Cathy was overcome by anger and self-loathing. Why did she always get the short end of the stick? The hand-me-down clothes. The ignored accomplishments. The wasted super powers on a mind too frenzied to control them. Even Fruit Man had beaten her in the random drawing of powers. They had ended up complete opposites of each other.

Fruit Man's body was an energy user, consuming enormous quantities and constantly demanding more—a disability that he seemed to have well enough in control. Cathy's body was an energy producer, with such an abundance of the stuff that she was incapable of concentrating. Every ounce she used was immediately replenished, giving her mind and body no chance to calm itself, to rest.

"Stoppit!" she yelled.

Fruit man loomed above Helen, enjoying each second of her plight. The crust had flowed down to block her vision. Bits of hair, like desperate vines, had wrapped around him, but what was free of the ooze was too little to do Helen any benefit.

Cathy wanted to cry, but her eyes would not listen. She tore at her hair. Why couldn't she have ended up with an easy to maintain sugar craving and Fruit Man with the debilitating sugar high? Cathy wished Fruit Man could have her disorienttation and confusion and not know what to do with *his* powers. There was a sudden clarity in Cathy's mind. The jumble faded and a single thought took form. Cathy took a deep breath.

"I'm the one you want!" She charged toward Fruit Man. "Take me!"

Kat and Danni arrived just in time to see the explosion.

CHAPTER THIRTY-FOUR
"Overloaded"

Helen

The shell that bound Helen had just covered her nose when its structure altered itself, erratic. The undulating sugar surged away from her in all directions and Helen sat up, coughing and gasping for air. Even as she rubbed her eyes, Helen was certain she was dead. She was surrounded by an aura of energy so pure and bright, that it blinded her to anything else.

A peace fell over Helen and she spoke expectantly into the light.

"Well, since I'm here, can I meet Patsy Cline?"

And the light spoke back: "Who the heck are you talking to?"

"God? You sound kinda like Kat…"

Helen felt hands reaching around her armpits. As she was dragged backward, she noticed the sludge around her legs.

"Are you okay?" asked Danni's voice.

"Danni, she's talking to God. Does that sound okay?" Kat flicked Helen in the forehead. "Snap out of it!"

Helen's eyesight adjusted to the glare and two forms took shape, silhouetted in the light. "Kat? Danni? I'm not dead?"

"No," answered Danni, "but who's Patsy Cline?"

"Now isn't the time for Helen to explain her religion."

"What's going on?" Helen rubbed her eyes again. "Where's Cathy?"

Danni pointed.

Cathy's unusual exploits had not ceased to amaze Helen, ever since their powers surfaced. Now, Cathy was suspended in the center of the kitchen, her legs dangling above the floor. The bright light that had convinced Helen she was dead was, in fact, emanating from her friend. Helen was in awe.

Glowing beams connected Cathy to Fruit Man. They flowed like rivers, and struck as lightning, shooting out of Cathy and landing in the center of Fruit Man's chest. He was on his knees with arms spread, taking in the energy with mouth agape and eyes white and glowing.

"He's draining her!" Helen wrestled against Kat and Danni. "He's taking everything! We have to save her!"

Kat held her back. "We can't get close to them, we'll be killed!"

"But she—she sacrificed herself—for me."

Danni cupped her hands around her mouth, tears welling up in her eyes.

Static filled the air around the kitchen and crackling energy spiked with wild abandon, surging every which way. Cathy groaned. Fruit Man roared. With one final burst, the light was gone and Fruit Man fell backward. Cathy dropped to the floor with a splat. Her friends ran to check on her.

Helen gripped her by the shoulders. "Cathy! Are you okay?"

Clear-eyed and calm, Cathy murmured. "I'm a little tired."

Helen yanked Cathy up and wrapped her arms around her.

"But I actually feel pretty good."

"Uh, guys?"

Danni and Kat had taken up flanking positions and kept watch on Fruit Man. He had drained so much energy from Cathy that there was no telling what he would be able to do. He was on the floor, still glowing with power, vibrating so intensely his form was blurred. He held his hands up, astonished.

"W-wha-w-w-what d-d-did-dyou d-d-d-o-o-o-o t-to m-me-m-m-e-e?"

Cathy didn't answer. She was staring at the floor, where she had drawn a smiley face in the glop. She sighed and smiled to match.

Meanwhile, Fruit Man's vibrating became a shuddering, then a jittering, followed by outright bouncing. He screamed.

"Ye-e-e-erg! Aaar-r-rg! M-ma-a-a-a-ake it s-s-s-s-st-stop!"

He jetted across the room, slamming into shelves, and sliding along the floors. Goo shot out of him from every direction as his body attempted to dispel the energy.

"Take cover!" Danni yelled.

The three girls dashed toward the lunch line, but skidded to a halt when Cathy failed to follow them. Fruit Man blew past her once, and the others sprinted back to grab their contented companion. They dragged her around the lunch line and huddled together, listening to the destruction nearby.

"What happened?" Kat asked.

"I think he...he..." Helen was at a loss.

"Overloaded." Cathy said. "I overloaded him."

The noise increased as Fruit Man crashed into more objects with greater speed, grunting and yelling the whole time. He was literally bouncing off the walls. The ruckus reached a crescendo, as the distressed villain burned himself out. A thick, sugary mist filled the air. Helen's nose stuffed up as she breathed it in, and she tasted sweetness on her tongue.

When Fruit Man's unwelcome energy finally spent itself, he settled to the floor and calm gripped the kitchen. Wary of the silence, the triumphant team peered out from the safety of the lunch line.

"Wow, Cathy," Helen breathed.

As it dawned on them that the coast was clear, Cathy and the other Space Takers crept out into the open. The scene before them was an alien winter landscape. The white sugary substance had settled, coating everything in the kitchen like freshly fallen snow. Their enemy's self-beaten body laid prone in the mashed potatoes, an unfortunate snow angel.

The girls moved forward, destroying the tranquility around them as they trudged through the sticky, wet sludge around their feet. Kat leaned over Fruit Man, nudging him with her boot.

"Is he done?"

Bubbles rose up around the sides of his face, popping in his ears. He was snoring.

"Oh yeah. He's done," answered Danni.

"We did it, Helen!" Cathy exclaimed to her friend. "We actually did it! We saved the school."

"We? We nothing!" Helen said. "*You* finished it. I knew we could count on you—that you'd always come through for us."

Cathy blushed a little. Her eyes shot to the side. "O-Okay."

"Now what?" Kat asked.

Danni said, "Obviously we, uh…um…"

The four looked at one another, bewildered.

"Should we just leave him?" Danni whispered.

"Neutralize him," came a stern voice.

The girls turned around, startled by the presence of some-one else in the kitchen. They had forgotten about Linda and the other lunch ladies, and they were amazed to see any of the once-crystallized women up and walking around.

"Neutralize?" asked Helen, shocked by the woman's callous-ness. "Isn't that going a little too far?"

"No nothing like that," said Linda, frowning at the older woman.

The remaining two lunch ladies came around the corner, wheeling a serving cart with a large vat. The vat was filled to the brim with an opaque brown substance which dripped sloppily over its edges. Whatever the substance was, despite having been made in a cafeteria, it was absolutely unappetizing. The ladies proceeded to hoist Fruit Man out of the sludge so he was sitting upright. A funnel was wedged between his teeth, and the lady with the brightest lipstick was the first to dunk a spoodle into the suspicious concoction on the cart. The determined lunch ladies began—perhaps a little too enthusiastically—ladling copious amounts of gravy down the small boy's gullet.

"Wait a minute!" Danni asked Linda, "What are they doing to him?"

Linda answered, "Oh, they are curing him!"

CHAPTER THIRTY-FIVE
"Was that a secret?"

Cathy

"**C**uring him?" Kat said. "All this time, there's been a cure?"

"My…" Linda eyed the four of them keenly. "You girls *all* ate the potatoes?" Without a reply, Linda explained. "The Generic Mashed Potatoes: Made in Taiwan were never meant to be served without the special gravy to neutralize any ill effects. For that I am sorry. It was I who allowed two scoops to escape un-gravied." She placed her quavering hands on Cathy's and Helen's shoulders and added, "Though I doubt anyone expected effects such as these."

She indicated the vanquished Fruit Man. "Or those."

"Is that really going to work?" Cathy had not taken her eyes off of the sputtering boy.

298

"See for yourself."

The lunch ladies stepped aside to reveal Tommy Walker, dazed and confused, but definitely not Fruit Man any longer. There was no doubt he would require a thorough scrubbing to remove the crusts of sugar and glaze, but his drooping eyes were clear of their previous cloudy sheaths of malice.

"Wow, his head is round," Kat said.

"Finally," Tommy mumbled. "Someone noticed..."

"H-he'll be fine." one of the lunch ladies said.

Kat looked at Danni, who looked at Helen.

"What do we do?" Danni asked.

Helen scanned each of her friends before her eyes came to rest on Cathy. She nodded slowly and deliberately. "The cure. Let's take it."

"Really?" Danni asked. "You're not gonna try and stop us?"

"No heroic speeches to convince us all to stay?" Kat said with crossed arms.

Helen shook her head, staring at the ground. "We did what we said. Stopped the bad guy. Now we're done."

No one moved.

Helen's body had stiffened like she was holding something back. And of course she was! There was no way Helen wanted the cure. After months of pushing and training, she had shown no sign of anger or regret that she had developed powers. Helen the cartoon fanatic and comic book reader.

Helen the team leader.

"Hey?" Cathy reached out for her friend, but Helen pulled away.

"What's wrong with you?" Helen yelled. "Isn't this what you all want? What you've been looking for?" She marched forward. "Let's go!"

"Helen!" Danni stopped her. "I don't want the cure!"

Helen spun around and stared at Danni, wild-eyed. "Well—well, too bad."

"What? Why?" Kat grabbed at Helen too, but the red-haired heroine was too frantic to allow herself to be consoled.

"It's what has to happen." Helen kept several paces back from her friends as if she needed the physical space to explain. "We need the cure so Danni can go back to the softball team. So Cathy can get straight A's again. And Kat can dis-appear or whatever and not be stuck with us nerds anymore."

Kat jerked her head back. "I don't want that," she whispered.

Helen didn't hear her, lost in her own tirade. "Dontcha see? It's my fault—all of it!"

"Long-haired girl," Linda interjected. "I told you, it was me—"

"No, it was your fault it happened, but it was my fault it happened to *us*," said Helen. She was breathing heavily now, fighting back the urge to cry. "I made you guys eat it. I dared you! If it wasn't for me, you'd still be normal! Of course, it was the potatoes—I knew it the whole time—the minute things started happening to us."

"Helen, no one blames you," Danni said.

"Well, now that you mention it…"

"Kat!"

"Right. No. No one blames you."

Helen continued. "It was my fault you guys were miserable, and there was nothing I could do about it. So, I thought maybe, if I made it fun, or useful, it wouldn't be so bad." She paused, eyes pleading for them to understand. "That's why I made you guys practice so much, why I made you do all this. I had to fix things as best I could. And then I hoped, maybe I did. Maybe it was okay now."

Cathy had never seen Helen, her fun and humorous friend, in such obvious pain. Tears streamed down Helen's cheeks when their eyes met.

"But it wasn't okay." Helen jerked her gaze away and back to the others. "I almost died. And what Cathy did to save me… she…she…I can't let that happen again. To any of you. If someone got hurt or…worse…It would be my fault. My fault!"

Cathy's thoughts were swirling again. Had her energy come back to ruin her concentration already? Helen's words and actions made no sense to her. Cathy had rushed in to save Helen, not destroy her. All her joy, all her confidence and determination had melted away.

"Yeah." Danni put her hands on her hips. "Some leader you turned out to be."

Helen scowled.

"A good leader wants what's best for her team," Danni said. "And right now, you're being nothing but selfish."

"Whoa," Kat said under her breath.

"It's like you said. It's not so difficult anymore. We have control. We're a team and we could help people. *You* made us that team." She pointed at the symbol on her chest. "I want to keep my powers. I want to help more people one day. And that's my choice—not your fault."

"You mean it?" Helen asked.

Danni took her hand. "I do."

"Yes!" added Linda.

Danni turned around. "What about you Kat?"

Kat put her fists in her pockets. "You guys really want me around? You don't know anything about me."

Helen wiped her nose. "I know you like cats," she said.

"I know you have asthma," said Danni. "Wait. Was that a secret?"

Kat glared.

"How is anyone going to get to know you if you don't stick around?" Danni said.

"You did come back and save our butts here, so this must mean something to you." Helen added.

Danni held out her hand for Kat. "We're the Space Takers. We stick together."

"We like you the way you are, even if it means you're eighty percent Morlock." Helen extended her hand as well.

Danni met her eyes. "And we won't leave you, Kat. I promise."

Kat considered Helen and Danni for a tense few seconds. She took their hands. "Alright," she muttered, uncharacteristically sheepish.

"Wonderful!" Linda clasped her hands together.

Cathy felt her stomach churn, like she would throw up neon bile all over again. She never wanted to hurt Helen, but she never wanted these powers either. *Please*, she wished, *Please just stop everything here and don't make me make this decision.*

The others turned to their remaining team member and Helen stepped forward.

"I'm horrible at this," Cathy pleaded. Her triumph over Fruit Man was all but forgotten.

"You're not," Helen said. "And you came through when we needed you. You always do. You're amazing! But you just don't see what we see. I don't want to do this without you, but it has to be your decision. And you'll always be my best friend. No matter what you decide."

When Cathy hesitated, Danni added, "They've got the gravy right here. You can change your mind any time."

"She most certainly cannot!"

The girls jumped. Principal Pal had scraped his tweed suit clear of most of the potatoes, and had skulked up behind them, cradling his megaphone.

"We have *got* to start looking behind us," Kat said, dryly.

"I'll not have any more of this—this madness!" he said, dabbing his forehead with a potato-covered handkerchief. "This is *not* calm. This is *not* orderly. No one is going to find out about this, do you hear?"

Helen tried to interrupt. "But—"

The principal stuck his bullhorn in her face and *mooo*-ed at her. He stalked up to Linda. "And you!" He pointed a rigid finger in her face. "You! —How? —Why? —Forget it!" Having nothing of any substance to shout at Linda, he threw his hands up and wheeled around. "We are going to clean this up here and now, starting with you four!"

"Give them a chance!" begged Linda.

"Yeah! We saved the school!" Helen said.

"And we saved your hide," Kat growled.

The lipsticked lady waved a spoodle. "There aren't any chances! This is it. All the gravy. This supply was meant to last the whole year, and then some, but we made it all to deal with him." She bopped the former Fruit Man on the dome. "We can't keep it around in case you fickle little girls change your minds."

Principal Pal pointed. "Now march! It's time for all good students to take their medicine."

CHAPTER THIRTY-SIX
"Real children?"

Cathy

It was one thing to fight the villain. It was another thing to out-right defy authority. With heads hanging, Cathy and her friends slogged toward the vat. The lunch ladies stood around it, ready with spoodles.

First in line, Cathy stepped up to the neutralizer-gravy, so gelatinous it jiggled when her shoe tips touched the drum. She considered her friends. Kat was fuming. Danni was ready to cry. Helen was empty. The sly twinkle in her eye, her constant smirk, both gone. This was no joke.

And yet, Cathy's salvation was staring her in the face. It was finally possible to go back to normal. Right here, right now. The pressure to decide was gone. After all, no one could blame her

Megan Cain

for following orders. So, why did her heart ache? Why did her salvation look so disgusting?

Cathy reflected on her decision to run into danger. That moment before she simultaneously saved Helen and damaged her confidence in the Space Takers. Helen thought Cathy was sacrificing herself, but that's not how Cathy had seen it. All of Cathy's thoughts and actions in that instant had been a jumble, an energetic blur, but something in her mind had broken through it all. The reason for everything she had endured had become clear and her own voice had told her, *If I do this, I can save everyone. If I do this, I can win.*

Confidence. Happiness. Knowing she was a part of something important, that her efforts were appreciated. That's what had flashed through her mind.

And she wasn't about to give that up.

With one fierce and defiant kick of her leg, Cathy toppled the vat of gravy.

The three lunch ladies shrieked as it splashed into the muck and splattered against the wall of mashed potatoes. A shudder rippled through the spuds as the gravy seeped in. The potatoes relaxed and deflated, gurgling as they settled down.

"Way to go Cathy!" Kat raised a hand to high five.

Cathy startled herself with an enthusiastic hand-slapping response.

"What have you done?" cried the principal, his voice a manic octave higher than usual.

Before anyone could make a move against them, Danni multiplied in size and snatched up Principal Pal and his lunch ladies like a handful of Marbie dolls. She dumped them in the walk-in refrigerator.

"The door!" Linda snapped her fingers.

Before the captives could rush out of their makeshift prison, a troupe of melons rolled into their path and flung themselves threateningly at the surrounding shelves. The captives retreated, and more fruits and veggies converged to smash themselves against the metal door until it slid shut.

"Wow," Danni said, shrinking. "When did the lunch lady get powers?"

"I always talked to them before, but this is the first time they ever talked back," Linda mused. "I'm so happy!"

Helen shrugged. "She did take a bath in the stuff."

"So, now she's some kind of vegetable whisperer?" Danni asked.

"I dunno. Those powers sound lame," Kat joked.

"I think they're cool," Cathy said, remembering their practice sessions from what seemed like ages ago.

Helen put her arms around Kat's and Cathy's shoulders, the spark back in her eyes.

"Let's get out of here, team."

Linda

When Linda and the girls clambered out of the lunch line, they were not alone in the cafeteria. Hordes of firefighters, in full gear, were rushing through the front doors. A man in a pressed shirt and tie stood in the center of the cafeteria, in awe at the state of the school he had come to inspect. He carried a clipboard, and a long beige coat was draped over his arm.

"Who is that?" asked the tall girl.

"Oh!" Linda said. "They haven't seen you yet! Change back into real children before they notice!"

"Real children?"

The girls looked at one another before doing what she asked. The bright aura around them vanished, and the four girls who had fought the villain and saved Linda disappeared— replaced with four identical, yet inexplicably ordinary girls.

Linda pursed her lips. "Who are you four?"

These new girls stared.

"Where did you come from?" Linda asked.

"Uh..." the blue-eyed one said, scowling. "We're the kids who saved you?"

Linda pinched the corners of her glasses. There was a tall one, a long-haired one, one with glasses, and one with sharp blue eyes—all just the same as before, but somehow not the same.

"Are you? Oh my, but you do look different."

The long-haired girl's face lit up. She squeaked, "You guys, we have secret identities!"

The clipboard man approached Linda, tiptoeing around the mess. He knelt and dipped the back of his pen into the mashed potatoes. They had engulfed two thirds of the room. As he studied his sample, his brow furrowed considerably.

"What happened here?" he asked as he stood. Then, to Linda, "Are you in charge of this?"

"I-I-I-I'm L-Linda," was her response.

"I'm here from The Institution of Public Education's Office of Student Nutrition, 'IPED-OSN.' Are you the same Linda who's been sending letters to our department?"

Linda took a shuddering breath. "I told them I wouldn't let them get away with this I told them I would act!"

"Is this…" he referred to the mess "…part of what you were planning?"

"Oh no. No no no no." Linda took the man's hand, and met his eyes in earnest. This could be the most important moment of her life, so she spoke as clearly as she was able, oblivious to the man's discomfort. "I outlined a new curriculum proposal. One that would teach students about food and where it comes from."

"Ma'am—"

"They could grow it and cook it and eat it and learn and sell it at bake sales and farmers markets and learn about that too! I bought the supplies myself but they fired me before I could harvest seeds for next semester."

"That's not—"

"I even bought sugar cane and corn to show them where their sweets come from which I think is important considering what just happened—"

As she spoke, the man's expression softened. He squeezed her hand. "But what *did* just happen? Can you explain what I'm seeing here?"

"Oh yes!" Linda dragged him back through the sludge, forgetting about the four girls behind her. "It started with a box of lies! Come with me!"

EPILOGUE

"**M**onstrous Mash Masticates Middle School." That was the headline on every news source.

The articles themselves went on to describe the temporary suspension of Pearson's Principal for ignoring staff reports regarding chemicals and expired materials in the kitchen. The missing students, Tommy Walker and Zachary Park, had turned up safe and sound, after a prank to hide in the school had gone awry. A diet of nothing but candy bars and snack cakes had caused fever, confusion, and antagonistic tendencies that had resulted in the attacks on teachers and staff. The boys would be allowed to return to school after counseling and a one-week suspension of their own.

As for the damaged kitchen and cafeteria, community-donated equipment would keep the food coming for the student body until repairs could be completed.

. . . .

Danni was trading Kat half of her sandwich for a bottle of orange juice when Helen and Cathy sat across from them, carrying trays of food.

"I can't get used to eating in the gym," Helen said.

"It's only until the cafeteria gets repaired," Cathy explained. "Should be done by the end of winter break."

"I don't care if it takes all year," Danni said. "As long as Fridays stay free activity, with half the gym full of tables."

"You mean you don't miss dodge ball?" Helen teased.

Danni chuckled and shook her head.

"So, how's the food?" Kat asked Cathy. "Since it's cooked on hotplates and skillets on fold-out tables at the end of the gym?"

"With Linda in charge, everything's great! I don't know how she does it."

"Yeah," Helen agreed. "It's weird, but it tastes good. Plus, that OSN guy keeps coming back to check up on things. Like Linda doesn't know what she's doing."

"What is that anyway?" Danni squinted at Helen's tray.

"Lemon-zucchini meatball, I believe."

"Ew."

"Try it, Danni, you'll like it."

Kat snatched a meatball. She put it to her mouth and they all laughed.

"Wait. Let's do it together, in case something happens." Helen stabbed a meatball with her spork.

Kat waited with her strange food. "What do we do now? I mean, we're a team, right?"

"A super team," Helen corrected.

"The Space Takers," Cathy added proudly, a meatball of her own pinched between her fingers.

Lifting their food, they said together, "The Space Takers!" before each ate her piece.

"Mmm!" Danni said as she chewed.

"Right, so do we go looking for more bad guys, or what?" Kat asked. "What happens to us next?"

"Don't worry about it, Kat." Helen counted on her fingers, "Principal Pal was suspended. Linda's got the cafeteria under control. The stinky henchman's been scrubbed. Fruit Man's been neutralized, and besides us, he was the only other potato freak out there. After all that, mashed potatoes eating the school, and an evil teddy bear golem from the bowels of the boiler room, what more could happen?"

ABOUT THE AUTHOR

 Megan Cain has never grown up. Oh, sure she might look like a grown-up, with a husband, a daughter, too many pets, and way too many real-life adult responsibilities. But then, why does she spend her spare time dreaming of super heroes?

The most important thing that ever happened to Megan Cain's writing career was winning a state young author's competition when she was nine years old. It was all uphill from there. Teachers should know better than to foster that type of creativity because she's been writing ever since. Thanks a lot Mrs. Dwonch.

Megan Cain currently lives in Maryland, where she hikes in the woods, hoards trash, and crochets geeky things, when she should be doing responsible adult things instead.

Made in the USA
Middletown, DE
16 November 2024

64284233R00194